To Li

*I hope these
stories will be
an inspiration —*

HERITAGE BUILDERS

HAPPY ENDINGS TO HARD DAYS

STEVE VAN WINKLE

HERITAGE BUILDERS PUBLISHING
MONTEREY, CLOVIS CALIFORNIA

HERITAGE BUILDERS PUBLISHING
© 2015

First Edition 2015

Contributing Editor, Lydia Howard
Cover Design, Nord Compo
Book Design, Nord Compo
Published by Heritage Builders Publishing
Clovis, Monterey California 93619
www.HeritageBuilders.com   1-888-898-9563

ISBN 978-1-942603-18-4

Printed and bound in United States of America

HERITAGE BUILDERS

ENDORSEMENTS

....

When you read Steve Van Winkle's stories, you learn that "Dirt" is not earth, a pastor's life is not just about Sundays, trout streams are akin to holy temples, and family is a trove of true treasure. The narratives in Happy Endings relate the life and times of just about everyone you and I know – we have all had our own personal versions of nearly every situation Steve describes – but it would be wrong to say, "Just move along. Nothing to see here." There is much to see, and there is good reason to linger over each chapter. Steve has done more than journal his own life. He has been busy taking life notes for all of us.

Keith Bassham, Editor
The Baptist Bible Tribune

Reading the musings of my friend Steve Van Winkle is a stroll through the Louvre of heartfelt essays. When I read "Happy Endings to Hard Days," I'm not really reading. I'm re-living. Steve's vignettes are his own, but they are also ours - just told better than we can tell it ourselves. Steve is a remarkable husband, dad, pastor, and professor (when he chooses to accept the lectern), and he is a phenomenal weaver of words. This work is life – with punctuation. Keep this book near wherever your best reading happens – your brain and your heart will thank you.

David Melton, President
Boston Baptist College

We've always been captivated by storytellers, from Moses to the Bard to Mark Twain. Their words move us to tears, light our faces with laughter, and then give us pause as we ponder our world and our place in that world. Steve Van Winkle is that kind of storyteller. He bravely opens a door on his life, never flinching from the inevitable painful moments yet always pointing us to the equally inevitable presence of God. In so doing, Happy Endings to Hard Days becomes both a companion and guide as we learn anew to trust in a God whose grace makes the crooked way straight.

Alan Pue, Ed.D
President of The Barnabas Group
Former Provost and Sr. VP, The Master's College, Santa Clarita, CA.

DEDICATION

....

To the full house in Montana that kept the broken one
in Nebraska from being the only one I ever knew.
Madison, Baylee, and Hayden, being your dad has been a privilege
that can only be articulated in words God has yet to give mortals.

Cheryl, only the words of the Apostle John expressing the futility
of trying to capture the scope of Jesus' life on paper can aptly
describe the scope of my love for you: "If it is written down, the
world itself could not contain the books that should be written."

ACKNOWLEDGEMENTS

....

This is a book that should never have been published, chiefly
because the author isn't the one who believed it should be.

That it has been is largely because of these people.
First, The Summit List of the Baptist Bible Fellowship.
This email list, populated by a spectrum of ~~loons~~ pastors,
was the incubator of almost all these stories; their reception of my
ramblings made them noticeable and introduced me to a joy
in writing my English teachers never could.

Next, this book is brought to you courtesy of Keith Bassham,
Editor of the Baptist Bible Tribune. Keith is the first person who
deemed several of these stories publishable; in the process of
working with him, he's become an old friend in record time.

Most of all, Otis Ledbetter singlehandedly made this a reality.
His encouragement and advocacy for what I have written has
been both humbling and mystifying.

I hope he doesn't lose his job for doing so.

And my mom. What else can I say? She's my mom.

FOREWORD

....

This is not a book. Well, it's a book; it was just never intended to be one. Before you read on, an explanation is in order. This is a collection of stories and thoughts written over a 15 year span. They were composed at different times and for varying reasons but with one intent: To somehow complete the experiences they chronicle. In other words, they weren't written chronologically and were never composed with any hope of being published; they were simply my way of tying up personal loose ends on the events comprising my life. Sometimes the only way for me to process a joy or redeem a heartache is to write about it; these essays are evidences of that impulse. I shared many of them on a private, pastors email list, which is the only place I ever expected any of them to appear; they were received surprisingly well. And, they caught the eye of someone who happens to publish books.

Over my protestations about these not being sellable and my not being an author, Heritage Builders Publishing has produced what you hold your hand. It is a collection of personal perspectives on almost-universal experiences; they were written entirely independent of each other. I remember hearing a band once talk about listening to recordings of their songs once they've finished in the studio. They said one person would always pick up a tone or note in a song never played by anyone in the band, but it always made the song better. Their only explanation for it was that the notes and instruments combined to produce their own secondary, unintended sound.

They called this a "psycho-acoustic." That is the only description for what happened when I went to compile this loose collection of non-sequential essays with no beginning nor ending which were never intended to be read all at once, let alone published: I noticed a flow of sorts I couldn't possibly have planned. It was my equivalent of a psycho-acoustic; even though the order and progression was never intended, still, it was there. So, this is a not-a-book written by a not-an-author containing individual stories written for no purpose whatsoever other than to be shared and (hopefully) enjoyed. Whether taken one at a time or a handful in one setting, the greatest accolade I could receive for ever having written them is for you to enjoy them.

On my best day, you'll be able to see your own life in them.

TABLE OF CONTENTS

CHAPTER 1

MOMENTS & HOPE

Summer of 68th Street

1978. I was completely unaware that June 17, 1978, was about to come crashing down on the rest of my life.

It was Father's Day.

Funny how we are usually driven involuntarily to the defining moments of our life and rarely allowed to meander up slowly. No one ever has time to "get used to" the car accident coming in the afternoon or is given a heads-up on the massive coronary about to claim a relative next week.

So it was on this afternoon. I remember lying on a broken-down burnt-orange couch, soothing a Nebraska sunburn. I had just gotten home from Boy Scout summer camp, not knowing the pivotal experience of my life was waiting for me.

The television in our living room was along the wall in which sat the window air conditioner straining to cool off the perfectly square box of a house we rented. Boxy brick houses lined 68th Street, like they were planted there along with the oak trees in nearly every postage stamp-sized front yard.

In summer on 68th Street, when it was too hot outside, reruns were the order of the day; the archived comedy of Get Smart and The Honeymooners seemed to help chill the increasingly abusive heat of June. Nothing, however, could cool off the explosion that was building down the hall.

In a home that had long before abandoned all hope of achieving Cleaverhood, a furious stomp and a determined, angry countenance was not an altogether extraordinary thing. At twelve, I had finally emerged from the reflex response of crying when my parents took verbal haymakers at one another. Even the trembling insecurity that always attended their arguing seemed to be quelling.

I don't know where I first heard the word "divorce." I only know the first time I ever spoke it was in the form of a question: *"Are you and dad going to get divorced?"* It seemed a good question to ask in the interest of my future, after the countless brawls that stopped being prefaced by "not in front of the kids."

Long before marriage counselors displaced the milkman in the vocabulary of families, this kid knew people couldn't live like what I was witnessing. When a child sees parents in disarray, there is an innate fear that bubbles to the surface and finds expression in the very adult questions unearthed in the eroding innocence of childhood.

I missed childhood.

The furious stomp and determined, angry countenance was from my mom. Clutching a piece of paper, she bolted in through the door, trying to slam it behind her. The shifting currents created by the swirling of the air conditioner made the gratifying slam of the door impossible to achieve, but that didn't slow her from taking a hard right down the utilitarian hallway to the last bedroom on the left.

The door slammed easily there, producing an aftershock.

My parents' was one of three bedrooms upstairs packed in an arrangement that more closely resembled the quarters of a submarine. It was where my dad had retreated for an afternoon nap. Insulated from open spaces by walls, the actual words thrown from an angry mouth may be obscured, but the volume can't be: You know when people are yelling.

My mom was yelling; she was yelling in equal measures of anger and desperation.

Sometime later, I learned that the piece of paper she gripped was actually a going-away card from my dad's now former comrades at Outboard Marine Corporation. He worked there in the credit department but, evidently, not anymore.

Perhaps even more surprising than the accidental discovery of her husband's unemployment were the people whom the card addressed. It said goodbye and good luck to Jerry... and Ruth.

My mom's name is Gaye.

Children never have an unobstructed window into the personhood of parents. To them, parents are machines sent from God to raise and protect them. Parents are the guardians of manners and the masters of foresight, and they exist only to make sure the children in their houses develop into productive contributors to civilized society.

Parents, in the mind of their children, never have events in their past, abuse in their history, nor plans for their future that are spawned by anything other than the kid's well-being. Kids simply believe parents exist on an island, secluded from desires and isolated from dreams and impulses.

In 1978, I learned differently. I think my dad loved his kids, but I think my dad's kids represented something different from a heritage, legacy, or even family. They represented a sentence—a sentence to mediocrity and predictability. They were the unfortunate consequence of having bowed to someone else's expectations.

Considering his life expectancy in terms of events, my dad could look forward to bland wages and tawdry imitations of excitement in a nondescript city. I suppose he envisioned himself renting a house forever or buying one which promised to be nothing more than another plantation for underachievers. His life would consist of insufferable monotony and end with a paltry retirement followed quickly by death.

Worst of all, between the slump into predictability and the certainty of his grave would be the endless, two-word question: *"What if...?"* No one wants to live with this mocking voice in their head, and my dad's was the first generation with a real shot of silencing the question his dad may never have thought to ask: *"What if...?"*

I'm not saying this is what he thought, mind you; it's how I imagine he thought. It might even be how I would have thought if my life were ordered by the same values.

After years of thinking about it from countless angles, I doubt he was the only one who dreamed of breaking free of the leg irons forged by his parents' expectations and anchored on North 68th Street. Of course, such dreams end up creating more casualties than expected; usually, that casualty is the innocence of those left behind.

It's hard to describe how it feels to lose something you never knew you enjoyed until it was taken away. On this June day, however, I was witness to the execution of my own innocence. Ward really does beat June. Andy fornicated with Helen Crump, and what Father really knew best was how to hide his drinking problem.

And parents sometimes act in disregard of their kids.

I don't remember how long they were in there. I suppose I thought this explosion like all the others would run out of fuel to burn, and things would return to normal, whatever that is. This was just a matter of enduring the turbulence of the moment.

But this was *the* moment. The moment that had been building since my mom and dad said, "I do." This was, "I don't."

When I looked down the short hall, all I remember is my mom walking alone toward the living room where I was. At least I think I remember it that way. I was in a moment where the big picture was overwhelming and the little stuff didn't seem to matter. I only know that somehow my mom told me I needed to go into the bedroom and talk to my dad.

My sister and I would go one at a time. It seems now like a long, long walk down that hall.

In my most lucid moments, I can only recall impressions of what happened in there, that and one sentence. I remember the arrangement of the furniture, the varnished pine slat floor, and that's about it for specifics.

I don't recall where he was when I walked in or what he first said or what I first said. I remember sitting on his bed and marveling at something I had never seen before: My dad was crying. If tears are the blood of innocence when it is stabbed in the heart, my dad was bleeding profusely.

I'm certain this wasn't easy, and I know if he could have found a way to do what he felt needed done without hurting people, he would have. In a very strange way I can't explain, seeing him cry at that moment has kept him human to me; stranger still, I've never been angry with him.

In that room, the only thing I remember being said was his explanation for what was happening. He told me he was going to San Francisco to look for work and he would come back for us once he secured employment.

None of which was true. Only I didn't know it then.

That one lie may have helped him get out the door with his sanity intact, but I still wish he hadn't said it. His false assurance of returning caused me to round the corner of Vine Street onto 68th every day of the next school year looking across the Vogels' yard and past the Helwhigs' house, hoping to see our truck in the driveway, tired from having brought our dad back from California to claim his family and start a new life in an undiscovered country.

Every day, I looked; every day, it wasn't there. Every day, I thought, maybe the next day. But there would be no magical "next day," just like there was no travel to California, no new job, and no plans to ever come back. There was just an intoxicating lie imbibed to numb the emotions of the one speaking it long enough to leave without a breakdown.

My mom, sister, and I stood in the doorway watching him walk quickly across the lawn toward the truck. No one spoke as the truck pulled away from the curb; we watched the brake lights flare at Vine Street where it took a left and headed for the Rocky Mountains.

A couple thousand miles short of San Francisco.

I didn't know that truck would never make it to California; my sister and I weren't aware of the details in the card. And, yet, it seemed as if I could feel each step our dad took away from our boxy brick house. They felt...permanent.

I think we all knew, somehow, that the Summer of 68th Street had just rewritten our lives. Forever.

Swimming Upstream

If you listen closely, you will hear something in certain people that's present in everything they say, but never more so than when they speak of their family. Some people can't help but speak of their immediate family as though they are pioneers.

They speak of forging a family without a pattern to imitate or a trail to follow. Laura Ingalls would find a camaraderie with them; they are pioneers of home who only know one thing for certain about their budding family: It will not turn out the way their parents' did.

In fact, I would say this is the majority report about families today; it's the reason so many people are marrying and parenting by instruction books and seminars. Why do "family ministries" blossom and why do "parent conferences" burst at the seams? Why do churches with strong family training and emphasis flourish? Because vast numbers of freshman parents and newlyweds are entering life having at their disposal neither a good example to follow nor a veteran of family nearby to consult as their questions multiply.

I was raised in a home that was dysfunctional not only because my dad had vacated the premises when I was 12. It was one of those rare cases where a dad's departure actually benefited a family. Not that he was a bad guy, just that he didn't "fit." In a family of four on the crumbling edge of Mayberry, he was the odd man out; his decision to leave was, I'm sure, for the best.

Which is not to say, however, it solved more problems than it created. For most of my childhood, we had problems wrapped up and thrown at us like evil presents on an obscene Christmas morning.

The worst of those gifts was the loss of innocence, as the world and all its cruelty and coldness walks in the door of a home opened by a departing parent. The jungle "out there" is suddenly "in here" and it has a profound effect on kids.

I think kids exposed to that jungle so early develop a dichotomy of personas. There is one that accepts life as it has been determined for them, adapting to reality and becoming skillful in all shades of impoverishment while mentally compartmentalizing the perpetual financial and emotional uncertainty.

Then there is the persona that surfaces only to architect the home of our dreams; it is a wander-ego that never relinquishes its hope nor gives up its search for an elusive place called "home."

That may sound a little silly, maybe even melodramatic, but I think you'd find it to be true. The search for a home that never existed is driven by an inescapable haunting constantly telling us it should have. Offering security without stuffiness, it's stable like a sunrise. Sunrises always look different in the shifting clouds of the new morning, yet the sun always comes up; it's always there.

This home is a place that is bounded on all sides by secure walls of right and wrong—the dos and the don'ts. After a lifetime of experiencing shades of gray and of bending whatever rules hindered their survival, these refugees are looking for a shelter from chaos and a sense of equity and morality.

This home is the place where the sounds of warm Thanksgivings, bright Christmases and sweet Easters drip from the wall like a kind of emotional condensation. Holidays here are holy because they were at home, where families would gather and not simply tie up long distance services and shuttle kids between custody agreements. This home desires to bless others, because the one who dreams of it senses an obligation to pay forward all the blessings they received from others' generosity.

Founded on goodness, framed in black and white, furnished in tradition, and roofed with security, the home of my dreams has beckoned me for two decades and continues to call. I think I understand why my wander-ego always drifted back to this place that never existed; if you had lived my life, you would probably understand too.

But what I am discerning lately is the sheer numbers of people who have the same desire, the same instinct. We are a generation swimming upstream to a home we never had but are determined now to establish. We are trying to reassemble what our parents saw fit to dismantle: A sense of family and community. I suppose there are many anecdotal evidences of this, not the least of which is seen in neighborhoods.

Houses seem to have "fashions." House styles come and go, and you can sometimes mark the eras by the homes in a neighborhood: This one was built when Ike was President... that one screams Watergate. But, until recently, they were all progressive. In other words, new houses were new not only in time but in design.

We moved into our first house this last fall, which means that we spent a good deal of time sloshing through neighborhoods. We must have appeared to be "casing" homes as we slowly drove through established blocks of houses, gathering tips for ours. As we did, something became apparent: The "new" homes looked old.

The newest, most popular homes built in our fair city are called "cottage style" or "craftsman" homes. You might know them as your grandma's house. Squarish, gables, garage in back, lots of shakes and shingles. These were the houses of the "old neighborhoods" when I grew up, the homes of the Archie Bunkers and the Andy Griffiths.

And while a cigar may sometimes only mean a cigar, I think there are some Freudian implications in these houses. From my armchair therapist's couch, they appear to be manifestations of a lost generation longing to go home—a home they never had.

What we are busy doing is constructing for our kids what we never had. We had houses, we had parents, we had siblings, we had good days and bad days. But we never really had a home, not in the way it was meant to be, anyway.

And we so desire to have one. We so desire the holiday table filled with whole families while kids eat on card tables with cousins. We want to show the world that home can be resurrected, that idealism born of harsh realities can be vindicated.

In a way, I think, we are also making peace with what our parents made war on: Home.

And this is a societal phenomenon that cuts across faith, education, and region. There are stats I could cite that would establish this, but, being born into this culture of divorce, I have all the evidence I need. I know this is what is being conjured back. We are a generation raised amidst the shrapnel of iconoclasm and the aching void of insecurity, and the only thing we know is that we will not bring upon our kids that to which we were sentenced.

Houses are not homes, but these new throwback houses are more like monuments to our collective determination to rebuild everything our parents cast off, to craft a new reality from our childhood imagination. It is the reality we spent the first half of our lives imagining and now constructing with the last shreds of our innocence.

We are a generation swimming upstream to a place we have never been before. It is a place we have only dreamed about.

It is a place called home.

Thanksgiving of the Exiles

On his last broadcast—well, his first last broadcast before returning to resurrect "A Prairie Home Companion"—Garrison Keillor reprised the most beloved songs he introduced on his radio show over the thirteen or so years the show had gone live to America over Minnesota Public Radio. He did them in an excruciatingly emotional crescendo of encores demanded by his audience who seemed unable to come to grips with losing an old friend.

The last of the encores was the PHC favorite, "The Song of the Exiles." It lyrically expressed the inner conflict all the fictional people who grew up in that beloved, mythical town of Lake Wobegon experienced after venturing out to bigger and supposedly better things beyond its shores.

Like all good writing, the song does more than that; it's evocative. Capturing the essence of longing most people who fled the homes of their youth have wrestled with as part of the terms of divorce from their homeland, it's mournful and puts the mixed emotions of all hometown refugees on display for the whole world to hear.

It's not that where these refugees are now is not good or even better than where they've come from. It's just that, maybe, home wasn't as bad as they once thought.

A critical hallmark of an exile that Keillor reveals so well is the halting retrospective about the places we all once called home. We bolted from the familiar decades ago with a sense of purpose or even pride. Perhaps it was arrogance or adventure that slung us out the back door of our homes, but whatever it was and irrespective of our resolve not to return, we sometimes catch ourselves wondering if it's really been that long since we left.

When we're off balance from such a notion, we often hear a grandmotherly voice in our head asking if it isn't time to "go home." Keillor's "The Song of the Exiles" put it like this:

"I looked back and shed a tear
To see it in the rearview mirror
I said I'd just be gone a couple months
And now it's almost thirty years."

For me, it's been 25 years since I left beautiful Nebraska, peaceful prairie land. I fled as if the milo and corn blanketing the state had a half-life and was rearranging my DNA by the second. Riding my own arrogance west, I wondered how any self-respecting person could remain in that place a single day longer than their sentence demanded.

In 1985, my future was not in a career nor even in a calling; it was in Montana. However, I would have gladly settled for anywhere not called "Nebraska."

Yet, the sentiment expressed in "The Song of the Exiles" has become the uninvited voice in my head. Thinking kindly of my birthplace in stray moments has happened far too frequently for a dedicated Exile.

My fellow expatriates and I are exiles by hardened choice, and the notion of returning is so surreal that we are stupefied that the very concept could be found in our head. Hearing it now several decades after leaving assures me that, no matter how far I've travelled nor how long I've been gone, a soft voice I heard from kitchen windows years ago will always ask me from time to time: *"Isn't it time you go home now?"*

I think every Exile knows exactly what I mean, or will know. Despite how happy and satisfied an Exile is in their second home, there comes the haunting feeling that it's been too long, that the limb is thinner than we thought, that someone is waiting up, keeping the light on for us.

That we've been gone too long.

All of which seems so alarming because we intended to be gone forever. More alarming still, the feeling seems to intensify at holidays, especially Thanksgiving.

It's partly why Thanksgiving in our home is for Exiles. We made it our tradition years ago to spend the holiday with people displaced from family for whatever reason. Initially, we simply wanted to be a blessing to those facing a day of thanks alone.

But *we* were alone; we had no family here.

We left our heritage behind in our hometown. Family traditions were casualties of adventure; the familiar scenes and the mundane people of our past were sacrificed for our future. At the time, we thought we would never miss them, yet we discovered their absence leaves a void in our spirit only those similarly exiled can fill.

Thanksgiving in our home is for the Exiles because none of us is immune from the melancholy of "The Song of the Exiles" on Thanksgiving or any other holiday. We love our new homeland, but there is an indissoluble connection with the home we vacated, and we recognize and honor it by surrounding ourselves with others who wrestle the same longing on holidays.

As we gather tomorrow, our thoughts will be on the numerous blessings we have neglected expressing thanks for this past year. But they will also be on faces and places in our past we discarded too casually when we were in a hurry to be gone. We're so thankful to celebrate with new friends, but we're also keenly aware of what we've sacrificed to do so.

We've been blessed in what we've done and whom we've met. Yet, for all we've accomplished and for all the miles we've travelled, we're now strangers on the streets of the cities and towns that raised us. It seemed a small price to pay back then, but it's a cautious contemplation now.

So, we get together with fellow Exiles, silently recognizing this holiday is more than blessing-counting: It is an homage. An homage to times, places, and people we chose to live away from and to heritages we chose to makeover.

As we talk together over turkey about places we were raised, there is a recognition once again of how our hometowns were personality blueprints as certainly as DNA is a physical one. We remember our families who mean more to us the longer we're separated by a handful of states.

In Exile gatherings, you'll hear fond chatter of things we left behind and people we thought we could live without. The conversations are evidence that, every now and then, we look in our rear-view mirror and see a place we once called home disappearing beneath the rise of our life and we can't help but think, "Isn't it time you go home?"

Thanksgiving with the Exiles reminds us of something becoming clearer every day. It is that we all hope the road we chose to take us far away from home will somehow lead us back to that place we know keeps the light on for us.

Over Time

A man in our church asked to see me in my office tonight...

I never told you about the "vote" on me as pastor, have I? It was easily a poetic ending to a good old-fashioned blood-letting.

Our church had been through a year and a half of interim during which we identified six men as candidates. Three never made the 80% required for a call, and three received the 80% and turned us down.

Eighteen months later, and after wading through human misery and sifting through the possible causes of God's evid hatred for me, the inconceivable became the kind-of obvious. I was the last man standing. I was a preacher in a church searching for a preacher.

It was, however, a church that was down to its last shred of hope, its last few dollars in the account, and its last few people in the pew. For eighteen months, the church and I both steadfastly resisted the notion of my actually being a candidate for the pastorate. In the beginning, the middle, and the end, I didn't want it.

I'm not sure the church wanted me, either—even after being without a pastor for a year and a half. My "candidacy" was more like a cold, polite handshake.

It's hard to explain, but this church was of the mindset that it deserved better, someone spectacular. I remember one of the men in a meeting over the stalled process standing and informing the church with palpable exasperation, *"You aren't going to get Billy Graham up here."*

That about summed it up. The people were looking for a man who wouldn't come here, primarily because anyone fitting the ideal profile was already engaged in a larger church for more money (yes, that often matters).

So, my candidacy was hurried and it felt hushed. It was like a couple people embarrassed to be in the situation and wanting nothing more than to get past it.

Which is what we did. We got it over quickly. Being on its last leg, the church's most critical need was securing a pastor—any pastor. So, a brief interview, a brief question-and-answer, and a vote were set.

During the Q&A, one of the questions posed to me was by a man whom I knew and who was, probably, one of the people you would say was looking for Billy Graham. He simply asked: *"Will you accept the vote, no matter what it is?"*

I thought, *"Sure, who wouldn't?"* and responded to that effect.

On the night of the vote, David Klass, a pastor from Montana City who had become a close friend, came down to oversee the affair. I sat with Cheryl and our almost-one-year-old daughter, Madison, in our apartment awaiting the result.

About an hour after the service began, David walked into our living room shaking his head. I remember his saying: *"I don't believe these people. What do they want?"*

Turns out I had fallen short by a couple percent. Even for a church that embodied desperation, I wasn't good enough. Not healthy for the ego.

But it was all right. I was ready to leave and, in all likelihood, would have wound up in Helena with David, which was a far more inviting proposition than having my first pastorate be a church profusely hemorrhaging from nearly every kind of congregational malady imaginable.

In a weird twist, though, no one had a key to the church that evening. This is strange, because everyone who DID have a key was there the night of the vote. All of them, evidently, had left theirs at home. So my last official duty was to go and lock the church since I lived only a few blocks away.

I walked in one last time and went into the spartan office; on a table, I noticed the pile of ballots received that evening. There I stood— e and the ballots of my first pastoral candidacy. Wouldn't you have looked at them too?

Some had messages scribbled on them, like, *"He's a good preacher, but we need more."* Yeah, I understood that. I was flattered someone thought I was a good preacher, but I was twenty-eight and the church could surely benefit more from a grizzled veteran of ecclesiastical triage than an intern fresh out of college. I think one said, *"He's not ready yet."* I couldn't help but agree.

It was another first in a long line for me over the previous eighteen months. As much as it stung to see every "no" vote, I couldn't help but struck how every "yes" vote was someone who wanted me to be their pastor.

Beneath the fluorescent hum of the lights overhead, I thought, *"Wow. What an honor."*

Just before I left, I noticed the piece of paper that tallied the votes. I turned to walk away and then turned back to see if I had read it right.

The church had steadily declined in attendance, so it was fairly easy to know the entire membership in my head. Also, during past votes, I was one of the people in charge of giving out absentee ballots to those who couldn't make the service. Consequently, I knew exactly how many people should be voting. The number was somewhere around 30.

The number of ballots received totaled, according to that sheet, 38. There were more ballots than people.

I called David; he called the Trustees; they called the Pulpit Committee. They met in the office that night and mapped out the auditorium, marking where everyone was seated. They then added in the absentee ballots.

Sure enough: More ballots than people.

How did it happen? I have no idea. The only way it could have happened was if someone voted more than once— unlikely, since the ballots were strictly controlled or someone with access to ballots "stuffed" the vote—probably wouldn't have been me, since I would have been more disposed to voting "yes."

That left one guy who was never accused and never confessed. I won't mention his name, but I will ask the Lord about it one day.

So a new vote was called. I had nothing to do with it; the Pulpit Committee called it. I didn't oppose it because I thought a vote should at least be fair. I was prepared to accept a negative vote, but I didn't want something shady determining my and the church's future.

Still, I didn't ask for the vote; I didn't demand a re-vote. I was just sitting home tying flies.

The phone rang. It was the man who asked me if I would accept the vote, no matter what. He was livid.

Seems in the aftermath of all this, a good chunk of people remaining in the church after those eighteen months were leaving. They couldn't stand going one more day without a pastor or one more day searching for one and some were pointing fingers about how the vote was stuffed. By the time I received this phone call, the people who voted "no" on me were fast realizing the ones who voted "yes" were looking to go elsewhere to church. It was not pleasant.

Like I said, this man was livid. He had that kind of voice that pitched higher than normal and quivered while trying to keep his rage from spilling out between the fibers of his vocal chords.

"You told me you'd accept whatever the vote was."

"I will, when it's a fair vote."

"Why are you asking for a new vote?"

"I'm not; the Trustees and Pulpit Committee are because there are more ballots than people."

"That wouldn't be necessary if you would do what you said you would do."

"Look, I'll accept whatever vote comes, but I want it to be fair. We're a corporation, you know, on top of a rigged vote being a dangerous affront to God, it's illegal."

His voice tensed even further: *"Hasn't this church been through enough? I can't believe you would put us through more. You ought to do what you said and leave."*

Click.

The next vote gave me, I think, an 88% yes. Assuming the excess ballots on the first vote were negative, this was about what the previous vote would have been without them.

There were major fences to mend with the aforementioned man, but it was a mending that only time could accomplish. While I was putting my books on the shelf in the wake of the second vote, he walked in my office like nothing had ever happened.

He sat down and said only, *"You have a huge responsibility now."* And he got up and left.

Over time is often the only way a person finds, not just vindication, but credibility. Over time, this man and I have had a tense relationship, more from my perspective than his. I wondered initially if he would ever support me and what I was trying to accomplish at the church.

Somehow, I knew he would leave. I expected him to make it, maybe, a week and a half. His wife was indifferent toward me at best and said, in fact, she didn't respect me as a pastor. Fun stuff.

He was cordial, but I was plagued with the feeling he was waiting for me to fail so utterly he could say, *"See? Told you you should have taken that first vote as God's will."*

He may never have had that kind of heart, but once a thought like that gets in your head, it ain't leaving.

Over time, though, the distrust faded and, amazingly, he and his family stayed. He became more and more congratulatory and more and more supportive. We have different ways of doing things, and we crossed and conflicted on many turns, yet, we've worked well together.

It's been a gradual but steady process. For the last three years or so, I haven't questioned his affection for the church and, really, his respect for me and what we've accomplished here. Along the way, I have grown to appreciate him and his unorthodoxy.

You're probably wondering why I had to tell you all this. Because it makes what happened tonight seem so much more meaningful.

This is the man who came to me tonight wanting to talk in my office. That's normally not a good thing, and when he mentioned it, I naturally thought, *"This is finally it. They're finally leaving."*

Hardly.

He told me he was about to sell his business. It was all but a done deal, and, once it was, he would have enough money for the rest of his life, which he wants to spend in some ministry capacity. The reason he wanted to talk to me was because he would soon be giving the church a very large gift and needed to let me know how it was going to happen.

Then he told me he wanted to give my associate and me the equivalent of about a year's salary.

Me: [Blank stare]

He went on and said the church has never had a better spirit than now and that he is excited about what God is doing, and he wanted to fuel the excitement in any way possible, with the money being the most obvious at the moment. I had been a blessing to him these last 9 years, he said, and he wanted to be a blessing to me in return.

Me: [Blank stare]

So tonight I sit typing as a way of testifying to the Lord's unimaginable goodness over time. Who would have thought the man who hung up on me because of that second vote that made me pastor here would have ever done such a thing?

Staring blankly some more, I was thinking not about money but about how far we had come from that phone call. It seemed I had been here a long time as I listened to him with my ears but revisited our history in my mind. And all I could think was, God, how can I thank you for making all things work together for good?

In the moment, you wonder if hard times will ever end or if enduring struggle is worth it. Over time, however, God's purposes are always worth waiting for and better than we ever dared dream.

The Last to Know

It was rainy. I had to unlock the door for her.

The foyer smelled of wet felt from the soggy indoor-outdoor carpet that hadn't yet dried from Sunday. Standing there with a nervous smile and forced friendliness, she spoke as if she had found a lost friend.

"This is Fellowship Baptist, right?"

"Yes."

"Great! I was part of Fellowship Baptist in Texas. You guys have churches down there, right?"

"Well, I guess so."

She was obviously laboring under the mistaken idea that we were part of some "Fellowship Baptist" denomination.

"Yeah, yeah...I love this church. I'm new here and I live across the street in the apartments over there." She held her hand out in greeting; I met it in mid air.

The "apartments" were subsidized housing. Bozeman has no real "bad" part of town; it has few poor. At least, the poor in Bozeman aren't obvious. Our church gave up assembling Thanksgiving Baskets for those who couldn't afford the extravagance of a turkey dinner years ago because we couldn't find anyone who needed them.

"Great," I said. *"Can I help you with anything?"*

"As a matter of fact, yes. I've got kind of a problem."

"Ok." My eyes widened, inviting her to tell me what was on her mind and giving a silent gesture of help.

"Well, I was praying this morning and the Lord told me I needed to get help from His people at the church I used to attend."

"In Texas?"

"Yes. Well, no. Kind of. You're Fellowship Baptist, right?"

"Uh huh."

"Well, I'm a member of your denomination."

Her persistence in thinking we were part of a denomination gave away the truth that she had never been part of any church, let alone ours.

"My TV is about to be repossessed. The Lord told me to come over here, and He said you'd make the payment."

[Blink, Blink] I was fumbling for words, which made her nervous.

"You're Fellowship Baptist, right? God said you'd make my payment. I can't miss Sally!" Her nervous laugh was snatched away by a smoker's cough.

"Sally?"

"Sally Jesse Raphael...SALLY?"

"You want us to make your TV payment?"

"Yes. I'm renting to own, and if I don't make my payment today, they'll come take it back. The Lord said you'd help."

"He did?"

"Yes."

"Well...He didn't tell me."

She went home. She accused me of being a "bad" Christian who evidently didn't care much for Jesus. I'd been accused of a lot of things in that foyer. It was the birthplace of the death of my compassion.

Years later, an older but able-looking gentleman caught me on my way out of the office. He was dressed like a cross between Grizzly Adams and Ghandi and strode up to the door with a rather substantial walking staff in his hand; I think he had bells on the tassels of his leather shirt.

He told me he was "The Prophet," just off the bus from Great Falls. The Lord told him we would buy his bus ticket to Billings.

I politely explained to him we couldn't do that, and he responded by stepping in closer to me. He glared and said, *"God told me you would buy the ticket."*

Over the years, I've concluded the Lord is spending a lot of our money without telling me a thing about it. I explained to "The Prophet" that until my Red Phone to Heaven rings and instructs me to do so, I wasn't able to give him anything.

As if it were possible, he lurched a little closer. I could smell mouthwash—a lot of mouthwash. Everyone working with professional drifters eventually learns that mouthwash is a kind of poor-man's Schnapps.

On the bright side, I guess if a person is going to be inebriated, fresh breath is kind of a plus.

"You will refuse God's prophet?" He drew the staff backward enough to be threatening.

I was twenty years his junior, a black belt going to my martial arts workout, and in no mood for a drunk prophet from Great Falls. I stepped in to him.

"Look. If Jesus tells me to buy you a bus ticket to Billings, I'll happily do it. When you sober up, or get rid of your super- chronic halitosis, if He still wants me to buy you a ticket, come back and we'll talk.

"But for now, I suggest you back up and try the Presbyterians."

Confession: I always send people to the Presbyterian Church. I don't know why; it just feels good.

These two incidents demonstrate why ministry types quickly become jaded about unfortunate people. It's necessary. Or natural. Or both.

Some people would mistake this for my hating people. Not true. What you will find, however, is that anyone who works with people has a cynicism to them that ordinary citizens don't. The last people to hold out money for anyone holding cardboard signs at an intersection are social-worker types.

It's mostly from experience.

Experience teaches young pastors very quickly that naiveté is very expensive. *"The poor you have with you always,"* Jesus said.

Pastors learn on the fly that there is an inexhaustible variety of poor: Poor in money, poor in spirit, poor in character, and poor in conscience.

Pastors are all easy marks, especially at the beginning. If I said out loud how much money I have thrown at sad stories and complete strangers, I think Cheryl might sue me.

I've bought gas, diapers, food, bus tickets, and even wired money to Africa after accepting a collect call that cost twice as much as what I sent. Truly, a young pastor and his money are soon parted.

Each time it happened, I was told God sent the person, the person is trying to get to a new life across the country, the person is trying to go home for a funeral, the person is trying to get to a new job.

Cheryl took a man—after his many protests—to personally buy him the gas he said he needed to get to Billings. The pump clicked off at .77 cents. With his kids looking out the back window, she put the hose up and went home.

I don't think she's believed a sad story since.

What makes us so easy to scam is that we tend to believe God brings people into our lives for a reason. Perhaps an idealism many can't understand, it simply reflects our dying notion that people don't lie to people who want to help.

I had this turned on me about ten years ago by a car salesman who, sensing my loss of interest in reaching a "deal," eked out, *"I'm not a religious man, but...something led you to this car lot."*

Seriously.

But we do, we believe in Divine appointments, even if they are scheduled by the Devil himself...

"I need you to pay these."

A tastefully dressed man in his upper fifties slapped a stack of bills on my desk. He sported a tweed vest, wore a groomed, salt and pepper mustache that matched his well-combed hair, and had an olive complexion. He looked like Professor Henry Higgins' older brother from Greece.

"*What are those?*"

"*My bills. I need you to pay them.*"

I had never seen the man before. His stack of bills was hefty and slid across my desk like a postal tsunami.

"*I'm sorry. We have very limited funds, and those are used primarily for people in our church who need help.*"

People tended to believe that because we had a building, we had lots of money lying around. And it was for them.

"*I need help.*"

"*Yes, but you're not part of our church. Do you go to church in town?*"

"*No. But I am a Christian; I expect you to help with these. I'm a student at the university.*"

"*Well, your expectations aside, I won't. Why can't you pay your own bills? You're a student, and you don't look like you can't work.*"

"*My back.*"

We then exchanged philosophies of charity for a few minutes. He was the most insistent man I've met about expecting money in return for nothing more than his wanting some; the lack of blush some people have when asking for "help" is embarrassing—they're always the ones capable of providing for themselves.

Still, many people think of churches like ecclesiastical ATMs and expect cash for the asking. We're happy to help when needs are genuine, but when people come in with demands, they're likely to leave with no more than what they had walking in the door.

He began to withdraw, accepting my explanation for our funding and even seeming to understand why we had a preference for helping those in our own congregation.

"*Well, at least we're all fighting the same enemy,*" he said with a secret-fraternity coyness.

Glad just to have him leave, I chuckled and said, *"Yeah..."* But something sparked my curiosity. I thought he meant sin or Satan or human frailty, but something made me ask, *"...Who's that?"*

"The Jews!"
"...Wha..."
"The Jews! They killed Jesus and they're behind all the evil we have in the world. Good Christians are always on the lookout for the enemies of our Lord!" He winked.
"No...Whaat?"
"We're all fighting the Jews!"
I had never actually met someone like this. I was stunned. He looked like a professor of literature, but he was as Nazi as any skinhead in the Idaho panhandle, and the only literature he seemed familiar with was "Mein Kampf."

A table separated us, *"The Jews aren't my enemy. Jesus was a Jew, for crying out loud."*
"Oh, sure He was...You're a minister? No! You've been deceived by the lie of the Jew. Jesus wasn't a Jew, He was Aryan!"
By now, his young son was standing by his side, having been sent by his mom to see what was taking so long. It sounds odd, but I resisted the urge to simply ask the man to leave, so his son could hear something beside goose-stepping propaganda.

"I feel sorry for you. The Bible says we all killed Jesus; we're all sinners. If you'd take some time to actually read it, you'll find that even the ones who personally nailed him to the cross were offered grace. I'd be happy to show you.

"The Gospel isn't about hating or seeking revenge on people who nailed Jesus to a cross. Jesus said He laid His life down and that no one took it from him, Jew or Gentile. You've got a very warped understanding of Christianity."
"I see; you're just another Jew."
"Yeah, 'Van Winkle' is SUCH a venerated Jewish name."

"You're nothing but a dirty Jew-lover. I suppose you have no money for Christians who need help because you're sending it to your Jewish slave masters."

"It's time for you go and take your Gestapo bills with you. I'd sooner light all the money I have on fire than give it to you. If you leave right now, I won't call the police."

He left, accusing me of being some sort of Jewish operative.

I only saw him once more, years later. He came in with more bills; I reminded him of our previous encounter and asked him to leave immediately. In Walmart that evening, I saw him pushing a cart filled with large electronics.

What's sad, I think, is that I started out caring. I wanted to help, and we wanted to show people God's love by acting in His name; caring grows more and more difficult with each episode like these.

I think most people want to care. However, in our business especially, you learn quickly that caring can be dangerous; just ask the widows whose pastor-husbands clutched their chest in their forties and fifties. Runaway caring can get you killed, so we frequently stop.

But just when we would seal off our spirit by slathering cynicism over every entrance, something happens. Something unexpected, something unforgettable that breathes hope on the dying flame of our compassion.

Like what happened yesterday.

Checking my church email, I fully expected to find nothing but the standard offers from exiled African princes wanting to stash their millions in my bank account. I was surprised to find an actual message from an actual person.

It was from a name I thought I remembered, and its subject was "Just thinking about my old church." I opened it and found this:

"Pastor Steve and Cheryl,

"You probably don't remember me, but I was a member when I lived in Bozeman from 1999-2001. I moved back to Alabama in 2001. I went through an extremely difficult time while I was living in Montana, but one of my fondest memories is how wonderfully everyone treated me at Fellowship Baptist Church...It looks like you and Cheryl haven't changed a bit, but I can't believe how big the kids are now. Time certainly does fly...

"Well, I won't go on and on. I just wanted you both to know my time at Fellowship made a difficult time easier."

I remembered her; I recalled she always wore a meek expression, like she was expecting to be told "no" even when she hadn't asked anything. She didn't do much here, didn't contribute much. She never taught a class. Mickey only came on Sunday mornings, hung out on the fringe, and was an Alabama fan.

Most of all, I don't remember doing much more than greeting her when she came to worship. Not once did she ask me to help her through any "extremely difficult" time; I couldn't even tell you what it was.

Mickey was just a pleasant person who spent an hour with us on Sundays. Until I got this note. Her email reminded me the best help is given almost unintentionally and that the people who genuinely need it are usually the ones who never ask for it.

Constantly beating back the waves of swindlers wearies generosity, primarily because it forces compassionate people to become bunco agents, always suspecting their kindness is about to be conned. But timely and unexpected assurances that my compassion has not been squandered because we never truly know how far it's reached has kept me from shutting down my heart altogether.

I suspect there are more Mickeys in our past than any of us realize, beneficiaries of our incidental kindness whose appreciation is as meek as was their request for it. In fact, because the world stands in constant need of warmth and caring, I have to believe people whose compassion continues as a going concern will always profoundly affect the world.

And I suspect they will be the last to know.

An Eloquent Gibberish

I could have sworn I heard the words. For 25 years, I heard things that I learned the other night were never actually there.

Every Tuesday evening, I looked forward to the tune with words that were very difficult to separate out from the hasty rock music. The ghost words I thought I heard were phrases like, "said to the bartender," "rock-and-roll in her heart" and "good love." Not that the words were important, the music was catchy; it was the only show with an end song worth a teenager's time to wait to hear.

If you know what I mean when I say, *"As God is my witness, I thought turkeys could fly,"* you probably know the song I'm speaking of as well. It's the end theme to the early eighties sitcom, "WKRP in Cincinnati." After an evening of Johnny Fever, Venus Fly Trap, Less Nessman, and Bailey Quarters (the inspiration for my daughter's name), I watched until the closing song finished up with the Mary Tyler Moore's cat meowing at me.

It seemed fitting that a show about an easy-listening radio station's transition to playing edgier rock music would lift an obscure track off an even more obscure album by an unknown band as its closing theme. For years, I wondered what group had sung the song; I couldn't find it in the credits.

I also could never figure out exactly what all the words were. Hearing them every week, however, I was able to sing along, mumbling words I couldn't quite make out and enunciating loudly the ones I could, which I mentioned earlier.

Turns out, *there were no words*. None. It was all gibberish. There was no band either, obscure or otherwise.

The omniscient Oracle, Google, is the ultimate answer machine for people lugging around childhood riddles unsolvable before the internet age, and it was time for me to finally ask about the mystery group behind WKRP's memorable song. Sifting through all the data it compiled in a fraction of second, I discovered the closing music to WKRP was actually just a demo hastily thrown down by a few studio musicians.

Apparently this ad hoc band only intended to give the show's execs a sample of how their future, full song would sound when finished. Because they faced a deadline and because real words weren't needed to give a "feel" for the concept, they had sung gibberish instead of taking the time to compose actual lyrics.

The execs liked the song the way it was, including the gibberish. Besides, they figured, a song with gibberish for lyrics would be a fitting, quirky parody on rock music itself.

But I heard words.

For twenty-five years I thought I heard words to that song, words that were only phantoms. A random selection and synthesis of syllables comprised of an intelligible but nonsensical fusion of consonants and vowels were what I believed to be lyrics, real lyrics—the kind with real words.

Google informed me the words I heard were never there, which meant I conjured them purely on suggestion. Staring at the screen, I wondered what it meant that I heard words no one ever wrote, words that no one ever sang.

Assuming a song would have actual words, I guess I heard them. Only I didn't.

Where do thoughts originate? From what spring do realizations flow? It's funny how completely trivial information can set in motion something as deeply personal as a moment of clarity, like the one I had pondering how certain I was of hearing words.

It settled on me that the soundtrack to my life has much of this kind of music. It "resembles" or "sounds like" a lot of things.

If people look at it, they can "see" any number of phantoms: Things that I hope they see, things they assume are there, things that might even exist in me to some degree.

I considered how easy it is to let the studio band of my life carefully compose gibberish, providing the suggestion of the person I want people to believe is there. If they looked beyond the suggestion, I feared, they'd see only a maestro too busy perpetuating the gibberish to actually compose anything of value.

It made me question the reality of what people assume is true about me. My clarity became very discomforting.

In place of depth of humanity, I can simply pose. The pose means nothing but looks compassionate and caring. Instead of faith, I can settle for constructing its facade. It's worthless for satisfying the spirit but gives the appearance of a man who walks confidently with God. Instead of a passionate enjoyment of life, I can orchestrate endless, nonsensical strings of platitudes about joy and optimism. But maybe it's only the suggestion of the person I want people to see.

The longer I live, the less people know me; they think they do because I lead them to believe so. It's hard to let people see us; in some vocations, it's as dangerous as a water buffalo calf flaunting a broken leg before a pride of hungry lions. So I keep composing a lovely, meaningless song that maintains the appearance of what isn't really there, at least not like it should be.

Get too close, however, and people might find it's only gibberish I have composed into an eloquent, nonsensical symphony of what passes for wholeness. Life is filled with so many responsibilities and so many expectations that it's often easier to skate by on appearance; it's not deceit, it's necessity.

People do it all the time, without even realizing it. We hint we are concerned, when we really only want to not seem heartless. We pose like we love our neighbor but never think of them until we're in need of their compassion. We construct the image of being ambassadors of hope, when we are chiefly guardians of our ego, constantly justifying our silence in a misery-drenched world.

No one is being disingenuous; we really do want to be all those things and more. But isn't it wearisome?

In my clarity, I also recognized how relying on appearance also thieves away joy and satisfaction. It's doing life as a dilettante, because no matter how eloquent or convincing the appearance is, it's still just gibberish.

It's a hard thing to face. Life was simpler when I thought that stupid thing was an actual song, but perhaps the first step to my legacy's becoming the symphony I want is recognizing the eloquent gibberish I've been satisfied with for far too long.

CHAPTER 2

....

LONGING AND FRAILTY

Remembering Jim

My "friend" Dirt was here this last week. Every now and then he follows through on his threat to come see me in between the paying jobs he only works twice a year.

He brought something with him this time beside 96 hours to kill at the expense of my productivity: a photo of my high school class reunion. Twenty years ago, I graduated from Lincoln East High School.

I had planned to attend the reunion if it was convenient; turns out, it wasn't. However, the photo was more than enough to resurrect memories of people I had forgotten and people I never should have.

I recognized very few of them. Twenty years smears the edges of our faces, changes the color of our hair and rounds us out in ways that can hardly be reconciled with a yellowing memory. A legend of sorts on a separate sheet helped me identify classmates two decades after I had seen most of them.

I saw old teammates, old girlfriends, and old objects of scorn. They all seemed well adjusted to life, and time had treated some very well. Seeing the faces, I wondered what they had experienced and even what their memory of me might be. I wondered if it would have been as surprisingly fond as mine was of them.

There was one face, however, I recognized and remembered over them all. It hasn't been twenty years since I spoke to or saw this person, but it may have been twenty years since I appreciated him.

His name is Jim Crew, and he was my first best friend.

Jim was one of those priceless friends that happen along so rarely in life. That friendship was struck when we were twelve on a shaded grass knob the summer my dad left for parts unknown.

I was new at being from a "broken home," and Jim, by comparison, was a veteran. Because we had adjoining paper routes, both our papers were tossed onto that knob. So, we saw each other most every afternoon that summer while folding the day's news.

Hot summer skies tried to pierce the shelter of our shade trees while we talked about most everything; I enjoy the memory of our conversations, in spite of remembering no details. A friendship was born in that carefree chatter under that shade, the kind that lives on even if not watered for years.

It's hard to give a tidy description to our friendship; it doesn't fall into neat categories. I don't know that we lifted each other up or kept each other accountable to any standard of conduct. In fact, we were usually together when I first did things that would bring certain wrath down upon my own kids today.

We were together for better things as well. It's these times I remember most clearly.

We were together with a couple of other friends, hanging out in my basement, when I was fourteen and the phone rang. It was a man from the church my mom had been forcing us to attend.

In fact, this man and his wife were largely responsible for our going to this particular church. His first name was Bill, and he had found Christ after a stint in the military that was, according to him, punctuated by drugs, alcohol, and violence. When I met him, he was a cleaned-up family man, and the only violence was in the reputation he and his family insisted was past.

When I answered the phone, Bill told me he wanted me to "roll" with him to his friend Earl's place. It was an odd request, but I knew him from church; he was as close to a family friend that we had, which helped me assume he was a responsible citizen.

Which, of course, is the perfect storm for finding yourself with a predator.

But I said I would go. Neither my mom nor my sister was home. When I told my friends I was leaving with a guy from church to go to Earl's and that they'd have to leave, they asked what the heck I was thinking, grumbled a little over the inconvenience, and left.

Turns out "Earl" was the Earl of "Earl's Tavern" on Cornhusker Highway in Lincoln, which is not the kind of place a 14-year-old should be found late in the evening. Or any other time of day.

Bill took me in, slurring something about how close he and Earl were, and we sat down as the conclusion swept over me that I had made a terrible mistake. My mom had drilled in my head that bars were places good little boys go to when they wanted to kill their mothers. While I wasn't innocent by any means, I certainly wasn't ready to cast my lot with the sworn enemies of livers that haunted this place.

It was dark, which helped conceal the filth, and Bill ordered us both a couple beers. An astute waitress noticed my lack of puberty, cussed at Bill, and turned to fetch him one. When she returned, he argued that I was "rolling with him" and was, therefore, entitled to a brew. She must have been a mother because her refusal was steadfast; however, she wasn't June Cleaver enough to insist my underage butt get out.

There was loud music and ugly people. A Mama Cass clone was hoisting a bottle in a corner of the hazy room and Bill told me to go ask her to dance. The suggestion was enough to make me consider wetting my pants; it seemed like a kinder fate than dancing with any woman there, let alone the largest.

After I quietly said no and suggested I ought to go home, he said, *"You know what I see over there?"* pointing at her.

"No," I replied, dreading the response.

"I see three hundred pounds of fun."

With that, he got up, walked over to her, and spoke words I couldn't hear over the screeching country music and pointed in my direction. She came to the table, and I danced with her. I remember this woman spinning around the room, but the whole thing seemed less like a dance and more like she was simply giving me a few minutes away from an obviously frightening experience.

Sympathy and help sometimes come from the strangest places.

Meanwhile, my mom had come home to find me gone. For some reason, Jim had stuck around and told her who had come to get me and that we had gone to "Earl's." In the time it takes light to travel an inch, my mom and Bill's wife immediately called Earl's.

Whatever she said on the phone convinced Bill to gather me up and "roll" back to my place. Pronto.

Needless to say, my mom was livid, flavored with fear. It was the kind of fear that prompts a mother bear to charge the hunter when he comes between her and her cubs. She also had Bill's wife at the house, who was visibly scared that her violent husband was drunk.

They yelled at each other; she accused and he defended his indefensible actions. I remember trying to calm the whole thing down. My mom was screaming, Bill's wife was screaming, and Bill was screaming while pressing forward over the yells of my sister and my mom to get out. Chaos would have been a relief.

Somewhere in here, Bill shoved or hit his wife; I don't know which. But the yelling had coalesced into violence, and God only knew what would be next.

More screams...crying...another shove...more forward movement into the house...my helping his wife up...my mom threatening to call the police. As everything was escalating, I decided there was nothing I could do but throw myself in the middle of the insanity and hope I survived.

The women were bobbing and weaving, trying to miss the assault, sometimes falling down; my sister was beside herself. When I was just about to take the plunge into the free-for-all, putting myself between Bill and the women he was considering beating up, someone outside starting yelling obscenities.

At Bill.

He turned from the women and started outside. I loaded a gun, took it to my sister and told her that if he came back in, shoot him. I ran out the door only to find Jim taunting Bill.

Being called a "*&%$##* p*#*y" by an adolescent has a way of incensing a crusty veteran. If I wrote out what he was yelling, people would have to send their kids to bed before reading on.

Suffice it to say Jim may not have been able to fight like a sailor, but he was no second-class citizen when it came to cussing like one. This night, however, his epithets were sheer poetry to me; he insulted this drunken ogre with the most colorful, crude, R-rated vocabulary I ever heard.

Jim also assured Bill he would kick his &^%$, but whenever he advanced to give him that chance, Jim backed off. The women were also screaming to keep away because Bill had hospitalized scores of others. There were a couple times when I thought Jim wasn't going to retreat; he always did.

The police came several minutes later. Bill in handcuffs was the last I saw of him, ever. At the time, it seemed like a minor blip in my life that was just beginning to be one great big blip.

Jim's expletive laced rope-a-dope was one of the first heroics I ever personally witnessed and my first close encounter with bravery. He singlehandedly kept my family from being a statistic on domestic violence charts.

The twentieth reunion I hadn't attended also reminded me of the night after our graduation, which effectively ended the closeness born on the grass under that summer shade. The next morning I was flying to LA with my dad for an unknown amount of time; it was one of those moments when life whispers that nothing would be the same again.

Our friends were down in the parking lot of Jim's apartment while he and I were on the roof. We sat alone looking down at them as if we were watching the credits roll on a chapter in our life, and we talked about the previous six years. Mostly the good things.

I can count on one hand the times I have had emotionally revealing conversations; in spite of the scarcity of words spoken, this may have been the first. When the memories had been exhausted, we sat silently for a few minutes; there were only three sentences left to say.

"I'm going to miss you," I said.

"I love you, man," he said.

"Me too." It was all I could eke out.

We threw our arms around each other's shoulders like when we were boys and went down to walk through different doors that lead to the rest of our lives.

Twenty years later, against all odds, I am a pastor and he is teaching in the math department of the high school from which we graduated. I look back at my life in a broken home and have often wondered how I never succumbed to so many of the traps and hazards that lay all about the feet of those shoved into such situations. I certainly know the Lord has always looked out for me, ordering my life in the steps of His grace.

Part of that grace, I've come to believe, was a friendship that didn't so much keep me out of trouble as it kept me from surrendering to it. In the years that claim so many victims from the poverty, premature independence, and bottomless confusion that marked lives like mine, I had a friend. I had a friend whose constancy helped keep me one step ahead of the disaster we flirted with together and reminded me that a broken home didn't have to mean a broken life.

There are probably twelve people in my life that have told me they loved me with a sincerity that dove beneath the surface; Jim is one of them. When I look back, I still believe it and am still thankful for it.

Some friendships can never be undone, no matter how long it's been since you've spoken or how far away you are from each other. These friends never really leave; every thought of them brings a smile and reminds you of the one thing that pays down the debt of gratitude you owe: Remember.

I remember, Jim.

Kisses in the Belly of the Beast

In 1996, my oldest daughter, Madison, was two beautiful and indescribably cute years old, and my youngest daughter, Baylee, was a squirmy six months old.

Yes, I spelled her name correctly. In a consequential moment of my absence, Cheryl was presented the paperwork for naming our second daughter and decided on a novel spelling of what I thought would be "Bailey's" name: Baylee. No reason for this spelling, she said; she just liked the way it looked.

OK.

April of 1996 was also when the church I pastor graciously sent us to Florida for a post-Easter getaway. Spending time with dear friends who had recently moved there and soaking in the sun while people back in Montana sloshed in the half-frozen mud and snow promised needed renewal, and we looked forward to seeing people who were like second parents to us.

On a particularly splendorous afternoon canopied by a crystal blue sky, my friend and I took Madison out on a small lake and spent the day catching sunfish. It was Mad's first time fishing and the start of what I hoped would be her following in my footsteps as an angling addict.

It's hard to describe the thrill of watching thrill consume her face every time she saw a glimmering little bluegill hoisted out of the water or when she spotted a small alligator darting under the surface (she called them "adigaytows"). The fun exhausted her to the point of an afternoon nap on the boat; it's still one of the best pictures we have of her.

To celebrate her day of fishing success, everyone met at a local restaurant that evening. When we returned to the apartment, we barely had time to sit down before our ears were assaulted by a sound from the kitchen usually heard only on animal channels.

The snarling and determined viciousness jolted immediate alarm through my brain, and I ran across the apartment to find my little daughter trying to get away from a very large and very angry Golden Retriever. She was leaning down to say hi to him while he was eating, and he attacked.

I picked her up and saw a ragged chunk of flesh missing from the center of her cheek, leaving nothing but an oozing hole behind. It was red and fleshy and bleeding and hideous and accompanied by gashes on the top of her head and around her eye. Paralyzed by a sense of surrealism, all I could do was hold her face firmly to my chest until my wife snatched her and ran to the car.

My shirt, along with the kitchen, looked like a scene from a blood bath in The Godfather.

The trip to the hospital was agonizingly slow; our friend drove while we sat in the back seat. Cheryl gently nudged

Madison to sing, "You are My Sunshine" with her. I had my arm around Cheryl who was clutching Madison to her chest now.

Looking right at me, Mad sang softly and cautiously but sang nonetheless. In the middle of one verse, she even managed to smile with me a couple times. Trying to appear as though everything was fine, I forced one back; her bravery, to me, is still without explanation.

The hospital was as busy and bustling as you imagine most metro Emergency Rooms. With one look at Madison's blood-crusted face, however, they swept us in and began urgently cleaning out the wound that consumed about a third of her tiny, once-perfect cheek. I couldn't stay in the room. I felt like a terrible dad, but I couldn't bear to see my little girl in such a mangled state and not be able to help.

Cheryl remained and calmed Madison with the high-tensile strength only mothers possess. I walked and prayed and prayed and walked. And wept.

When I finally came back, the plastic surgeon was there. He said there was little he could do except clean out the big wound and stitch up the 4 others he could see. As far as "good news" went, he assured us the long gash on top of Mad's forehead that lurched down to her nose would recede into her hair as she grew, and that the smaller cuts would scar less now than they would have if this had happened later in life.

"Good news" about savagery is never good enough. It's like someone who's lost a leg being consoled by someone assuring them that now is a much better time to lose one than a few years ago because today's prostheses are so advanced. It's good news but not really.

Finally, he said the gaping hole in her cheek would have to stay open. What's hard to grasp in the moment is that a bite is unlike a cut in that a cut is simply a separation of tissue that can be rejoined with sutures. A bite, however, removes tissue and can't be rejoined because it would deform the surrounding area, like cutting a hole in a sheet and sewing it together: It never lays right again.

For the foreseeable future, we would have to clean it out with peroxide every day and re-bandage it until a scab filled in the gap.

Then, he said something that helped me ease out of the swelling tide of anger and depression beginning to consume my thoughts. He told us we were in for a long haul and that the worst was yet to come, but he also said he was utterly amazed at what didn't happen.

The hole went down to the tissue of the mouth, but didn't penetrate it. The dog's teeth grazed the medial nerve that controls the mouth (smile, etc.) but didn't sever it. There were several bite marks around the left eye but none that struck it. Most of all, the bite occurred only one inch from her jugular vein; it could easily have been on the throat, killing her nearly instantly, but wasn't.

We went back to the apartment. Madison's face looked like she had been beaten by angry chimps with lead pipes. Her entire two-year-old face was bruised; one eye was almost swollen shut. The tracks of stitches laid on her forehead and cheek and near her eye looked like macabre zippers on her flesh, and she was wound up with gauze on her head to keep the hole covered from infectious germs.

That thumbnail-sized hole was where I had kissed her little face so many nights as she slipped into sleep. It seemed that the kisses I planted there were now in the belly of a beast that had savagely maimed my little daughter to protect his dog food.

From questions of why to impulses of revenge to the self-flagellation of questioning how I could have prevented the entire thing, anger and depression were swelling again.

Cheryl gathered Madison and Baylee to herself and went to bed. A couple nightmares from Mad followed and I don't even remember if I went to sleep. Instead of lying down, I turned on the TV and tried to forget what happened.

Turns out, what happened to us had happened on the second anniversary of the Oklahoma City bombing. The lead-in to Nightline was the famous, gut-wrenching picture of the fireman forlornly staring down at a little baby whose lifeless limbs dangled from her lifeless body.

I never knew what that baby's name was until then. Her name was Baylee. Yes, I spelled it correctly.

At that moment, my perspective changed. Instead of wondering why God hadn't prevented what happened to my precious daughter, He helped me understand His mercy to me in what He *didn't* allow to happen.

In that chair, with the occasional cry from Madison on being wakened by a nightmare, I thought how somewhere out there was a family whose Baylee was snatched away from them in a senseless, pointless plot hatched by two men no one had heard of to prove a point no one cared about. My Baylee, along with her wounded older sister, was fine, and both were now safe in the arms of their mother.

Why was I spared when others had faced a darkness I didn't want to acknowledge existed? This was a moment when I felt the weight of God's grace in my life.

I had to preach that Sunday after only a couple days off the plane from Florida. I spoke from Lamentations 3:19-26 and entitled the sermon A Quiet Hope. The thought was taken from how Jeremiah responded to the fall of his beloved city and the brutality that ensued. In the midst of witnessing unspeakable horrors as the Babylonians raped and enslaved an entire civilization, the Prophet says something almost out of time: *"It is of the Lord's mercies that we are not consumed, because His compassions fail not."*

I told our people how Jeremiah's ability to respond with humility at God's devastating work amazed me. Reading it, I had come to see how, even in the tragedies of life, God's mercies are inevitable. The last lines of this handwritten sermon are these:

"The events of the past week in our family have been screaming for an outlet. Jeremiah, perhaps better than most, could appreciate how delicately our lives are balanced by the grace of God. I suppose by 'the delicate balance of life' I refer to the limitless potential for daily disaster in our little worlds.

"Every day there are countless opportunities for tragedy, and yet 99% of them are never realized. Each day passes in relative anonymity and blurry familiarity. But when the scale is tipped in one direction or another, things come into focus fast. Let me share with you what the Lord has shown me in our personal disaster: Tragedy can consume your life or cause your blessings to stand in stark relief."

I shared with them how God spared me by protecting my little girl from what could have been. Only then did I understand that even the sound of a little girl startled by nightmares was a reminder of how good He had been to me: I could have had nothing to listen to and no one to comfort.

With that, I think I also understood Jeremiah. Perhaps his praise for God's unfailing mercies and compassion in a moment when neither seemed present was the result of the prophet grasping what could have been: They could have been captured, tortured, enslaved, AND cast off by God.

Late in the night of the second anniversary of a bomb that killed someone else's Baylee, mine, her sister Madison, and my wife Cheryl were sleeping in the room behind me. In that chair, I rehearsed again the list of horrors the hospital surgeon marveled had NOT happened, and I was seized by a simple idea.

It was that, oftentimes, only in considering what could have been are we humbled by how good God actually has been.

The Sweet Smell of Fall

Have you ever walked along the concrete on a glorious fall day to be surprised by the scattered crunch of dry, painted leaves beneath your feet? Too often sneaking up on people before they make the conscious choice to enjoy it, fall is best sipped intentionally by people who enjoy a little luxury in their seasons.

While other seasons freely exchange varying shades of familiar greens, whites, and grays, fall has its own patented colors. As the earth begins to tilt away from the sun, God awakens people who have been lulled to sensory sleep by summer's monotonous, cloned days with a new palette of dazzling colors unavailable to the other three.

Streaked with sleek silvers and washed-out purples and smeared, wispy clouds, fall skies have a depth without equal. Unlike summer, which remains aloof, fall seems to try to touch humanity.

These months smell like life, even more so than spring. Spring is life idealized; fall is life as it is. The sweet mingling of both the living and the dying flowing together jolts sleeping spirits into vitality with a beauty explainable only by a Creator Who delights in delighting His creation.

It's a season when things which only weeks before were healthy and enjoying summer's caress are now dealing with the fleeting days of life. I can't help but think, unlike in any other season, there is a message from the Lord reminding us of the boundaries of our time here.

Fall takes people in the middle of their personal summers when health thrives, opportunities are plentiful, and activity abounds and taps them on the shoulder and, as Solomon wrote in Ecclesiastes, whispers through splendor for us to, *"...remember the days of darkness, for they shall be many."*

The summer of life seduces us into perceiving time as a deep, bottomless reservoir on which we lounge endlessly and not a flowing river carrying us to a destination. Deceived by this gentle lie, the moments we can never recapture are delayed, believing there will always be time. A date with a lovely daughter, a simple card to a taken-for-granted spouse, a thank-you to a loving friend, a prayer to our faithful God are all urgencies that life's summer anesthetizes us into doing on some mythical "tomorrow."

Fall is a wake-up for those who are attentive to life's flow, telling us that what we need to do, we should already have done. Still, it's also forgiving enough to provide the time needed to seize the best things before winter steals away our opportunity.

Autumn, in its essence, is about dying; it reveals how the end should come. Dignity. Beauty. Style. But instead of mourning its own end with sudden grays and instant lifelessness, the landscape settles into the necessity of its departure and offers up brilliant reds, iridescent yellows, deep oranges, and spectacular combinations of all three. Fall is determined to be a blessing as long as it can hold on.

Which makes it the perfect blueprint for living out the end of our days: Never quit until you can go no more, and exit life leaving behind a wake of beauty. The quiet dignity in the fading life of fall displays the truth that God will do what He does when He wants, and the best we can hope for is to be a blessing throughout our journey.

Splendorous bursts of color at a time when death could be quietly and mournfully slipped into shows us that the end of our lives should be the most active in terms of beauty and blessing to others. Just as the leaves of autumn have nothing to gain themselves by displaying their true brilliance, such selflessness in our generosity and blessings when we have nothing left to gain from dispensing either will make for a life well-remembered.

The beauty of the autumn leaves was there all along, but summer masked the brilliance beneath a layer of chlorophyll. Fall, with its shorter light and cooler air, unmasks the true colors of the foliage, and it leads us to be thankful for the time they have been with us, enjoying every minute they remain.

Shouldn't the end punctuation of our lives be this beautiful? While laboring within the obscurity of our summer days, we should be looking ahead now and then to when our labor will cease and our legacy will shine forth—a legacy that is here right now, hidden beneath summer's busyness.

Paul tells Timothy that the good works of men "are manifest beforehand and they that are otherwise cannot be hid." When our autumns arrive, what will they unveil about our legacy, what will it be that "cannot be hid?" A life of unmistakable beauty shining through can't be hastily manufactured in the end; it must be wrought all along the way.

The sweet smell of fall is of gentle reminders and graceful goodbyes. But perhaps most of all, it is a lesson about time. Time to heed the reminders and architect the goodbyes. It is about time to accomplish what summer lulled us into putting off and winter will not allow us to finish.

The sweet smell of fall is the aroma of a life lived well and ending even better.

Christmas Comes Anyway

12/15/06
"Well ... I hate people ..."
I don't journal much. Not as much as I would like, anyway. I've never been that disciplined to sit down daily and write about my life, and somehow, I think private thoughts should be private.

That's the Midwesterner in me.

Besides, a journal seems like a scandal in waiting. I always live in fear that if I let my private reflections see the light of day, even if they are in a journal, someone will find them and read them and then ... well ... badness.

This isn't to say that I never journal. I have one; I write in it occasionally when the mood strikes or when I am in an unusual flow of ambition. Last year about this time I had that fleeting ambition to chronicle my musings about events in life and church, and I looked back the other day on what I wrote over the Christmas season last year.

It's not Hallmark material. The above quote pretty much sums up how I felt ten days before the event.

Christmas '06, for me, was mired in a church malaise that threatened to drain the holiday of any beauty it possessed. The story will be familiar to anyone in church for more than a couple years: Some things change in church and some people can't. The result is not something you can hang on a tree or would want adorning your porch on winter's frigid evenings. It's something incongruous with the spirit of the season, like a chicken suit at a funeral.

It's misery.

There aren't many Christmas tales about misery. There aren't many yuletide yarns about abject discouragement or carols about burning disgust. In fact, so often in popular culture, Christmas is not about life or reality at all. It might end in reunions or it might be about warm lessons or it could be built on children's idealism. It's certainly the place memories dwell.

But, it's not about misery. Which means that Christmas and I didn't have much to talk about last year at this time.

Funny, when things in life are not right, arbitrary dates set on the calendar are not anticipated so much as dreaded. The atmosphere of my life leading up to Christmas last year was equal parts frustration and foreboding. "Hate" was the only word I could find at the time, and it rendered every holiday smile contrived and every card suspicious and all celebration excruciating.

12/19/06

"The saga continues ... Now I've heard a rumor that one of our families is leaving. For history's record: Never once has either of them mentioned leaving or mentioned having a struggle ... I can't understand ... Trading in years of relationships without even a conversation ... With everything good left to accomplish in the world, the most trivial of incidentals are what people separate over."

I would have happily paid the Grinch to steal Christmas '06, only the substance of this particular holiday wouldn't have been worth the effort to tie an antler on that poor mutt's head. As it drew near, the celebration seemed pointless. The glitter of tinsel and warmth of lights were more a mockery of the season than anything.

All the things I have enjoyed since I was a kid reminded me of all Christmas wasn't this year. It wasn't fun; it wasn't meaningful; it wasn't hopeful; it wasn't comforting; it wasn't joyful. It wasn't ... Christmas.

It was any other day, any other month. December slogged on like it was March. March is wet, damp. March is soggy feet and muddy yards and dreary sunsets and forgettable dawns. March is the month-equivalent of gray. December 19 felt like March 19: forgettable weather with no point to the season at all.

When life strips Christmas of its wonder, December is nothing more than another March. Only you have to wait longer for the splendor of June.

And that's what life had done. Turning Christmas into another annoying season to endure and not an event to celebrate, it scoured my spirit clean of optimism, filled it with futility and managed to make everything about the holiday seem shrill and tawdry.

Life had managed to depose Christmas and enthrone reality. Hard, cold and hopeless, reality ruled December '06 like a tyrant at war with hope.

12/20/06

"In spite of it all, I WILL enjoy Christmas..."

I remember in these words a childlike determination, not so much of the noble variety but of the delusional variety. It was the kind of determination people muster when they exclaim, *"I WILL enjoy my root canal."* You know you won't, but you're upset that you can't.

Defiance of what can't be changed often borders on the irrational, which is what these words conjure in my memory. They are my defiance to the truth that I would do no such thing at Christmas; I would not enjoy it.

I would, however, have to endure it. I'm a Christian. I'm a pastor. I can't skip Christmas. I can't pretend it isn't there. In many ways, I am the face of Christmas. It might as well be in my contract, which I don't have.

And endure it I did. I endured the sermons I preached. I endured the carols we sang. I endured the festivities and parties we hosted and attended. I endured the programs at church. I smiled, I sang, I preached. I endured everything while drowning in contention and sadness.

What I wrote in my journal was not what I knew in my heart. In my heart, I wanted this fraudulent season to end, so we could get on with the rancor at hand.

12/28/06

"Everything over ... Christmas Eve had over 20 people at the house ... It was a very fun evening with chili and homemade eggnog ... Very festive. The real 'fun' of Christmas, it seems, is the fellowship with others and kids ... I don't know what Christmas

was like before we started having others over ... It is so much better when shared."

And there it was.

I can't say that it's inspiring prose or even an inspiring thought, but, as I wrote those words, I understood that life doesn't always schedule madness and petulance and discouragement around Christmas. Looking back on it, I find that though life may make Christmas very inconvenient, Christmas comes anyway.

Christmas invaded our home with the warmth of Christian fellowship and human kindness and melted the calluses of adulthood with the innocence of children's wonder. Disgust and frustration about my present situation were overcome by traditions that reminded me of all that has been good about Christmases past.

In December of 2006, I dreaded the approach of Christmas. And Christmas came anyway.

It always has.

Christmas came anyway to Bob Cratchit's family, even though old Mr. Scrooge had fired him the day before. Facing destitution, Christmas descended on the house and refused to be put off by the desperation.

Christmas came anyway to bloody Flanders Fields in World War I. Bringing peace to no man's land, it allowed combatants to lay down arms and sing carols with one another as Christmas trees popped up in the festering misery of the trenches.

Christmas came anyway in my home when I was a kid and our family probably couldn't "afford" Christmas. Christmas doesn't care if it is financially feasible; it has never cared about the gifts or the extravagance of the decorations. Christmas comes anyway.

Christmas came to the world originally in spite of not being asked and in spite of the tyranny of Rome and the upheaval in Palestine. Christmas came to a young couple that could scarcely understand the meaning but embraced the call to sacrifice.

Christmas came in spite of our sin, as it spilled into a world of darkness with unspeakable light; it requires no preparation. Christmas comes anyway.

And Christmas came last year to my life, but not as a boisterous celebration nor in the wake of elaborate programs. It came subtly but inevitably. In the company of friends and in the exuberance of my kids, Christmas arrived. Not caring about my lack of "spirit" or my struggles with people, Christmas came anyway.

In good times and worse times, as individuals or as a creation, we need the sublime words to wash over us, *"For unto you is born this day, in the city of David, a Savior which is Christ the Lord ... Glory to God in the Highest and on earth, peace, good will towards men."*

Opportunities to find despair and discouragement in the course of living abound; we need Christmas and its hope of life in Christ to remind us there is more. Precious more.

Browsing my journal, I'm assured that Christmas doesn't care if it can be afforded or if it is good timing or if we are prepared for it or if it makes sense or even if it will be observed at all. Because it has to, because we need it to, Christmas comes anyway.

The Last Lesson

My summer began with my trying my very best to land myself in a treatment center for those with Xanax and Ambien dependencies, both of which I consumed in quantities seemingly large enough to sedate an elephant until my grandchildren retire. These potions were prescribed by our doctor for my flight with

14 of our church people on a Mission Trip to South Africa, the opposite side of the planet from Montana.

I don't like to fly.

People have asked me about it and why I haven't written anything yet. The only thing I can say, admitting that it sounds melodramatic, is that the experience seems almost too personal to share.

When I say it was nothing like what I envisioned, nothing could be more accurate. My time there transcended the pastor-traveling-to-the-mission-field-for-photo-op thing. I was confronted with my life. I was slapped with my own days. There really is another side of the world. It really does exist in more than pictures.

And it can really make you feel very small.

I was expecting to get to South Africa and see a new culture, preach, and see throngs of Africans come to Christ. I was expecting to see quaint people in love with Jesus in huddled churches enjoying the fellowship of Christ. I was expecting God to speak to me about how much the gospel is needed around the world and to badger me about going somewhere and doing something about it.

What I found was ambivalence to a message that has been preached and re-preached and even re-created to the point that Christianity, if not the gospel, is as familiar in the farthest reaches of South Africa as it is in Chattanooga. Sure, we preached; sure, we preached in unusual settings; sure, people were saved ...

[Journal entry]—*"[The house where service was held] was at the back side of a dead-end road which seemed to roll off a mountain ... the house was down a trail we could not see in a place we could only hear ... Beautiful sight, though ... from where we preached, we could see the lights of the city of Durban off to our right and the Indian Ocean coast blackness on our left. A vast strip of darkness separated the lights of Durban. The missionary said this was the 'no-man's land' that partitioned Whites from Blacks during Apartheid."*

... but what I found was a country so saturated with "Christianity" that the greatest missionary need seems to be to save people from errant forms of it.

[Journal Entry]—*"People still believe that Africa is spiritually dark in that it has not heard the gospel, but the opposite is true ... It is spiritually dark, because it's filled with a corrupted gospel."*

What I found was gracious, friendly people who touched my life, seemingly hardened somewhat by the conditions of their existence. Crime, AIDS, and myriad manner of other human stenches are a daily companion in this place ...

[Journal entry]—*"At McDonald's, after the service, Tembeh (one of the Missionary's national leaders) looked at me and said, 'You miss your home, don't you?' ... I had given up hiding that emotion and told him that actually I missed my family ... truth is, though, that I'm beginning to think of these guys as friends and wonder what it will be like to never see them again ... I hope I do."*

And while the people are incredibly friendly, there is a look in their eyes that speaks to a certain battle-weariness with life. People who live in a simplicity dictated by poverty and consider a "step-up" what I perceive as abject misery and want.

[Journal Entry]—*"The house was even smaller than I expected ... main room is maybe half the size of my living room with a toilet and shower in the space of our half-bath and one sink off the main room ... wires draped from the ceiling carrying power to light bulbs hung naked and loosely from the wall. Before getting a slightly larger house, the owner lived there with her daughter and four grandchildren."*

Even more shamefully, I touched the hem of prejudice. Not black and white but American / world ... I wrestled at times with the superiority that attends being raised in the land of the free and the home of the brave.

[Journal Entry]—*"People along roads with nothing to do but be along a road ... numerous nationalities, truly an international place ... saw 'informal settlements' today: shacks, basically, constructed from cardboard, tin, plastic, trash ... literally look like houses made of trash, about the size of a small shed and erected on any open land available ... Hard to describe reaction to it ... wanted to see third-world poverty but wasn't really prepared. Wish I could say I felt overwhelming compassion, but it was more like insecurity ... Think I finally realized I was in a foreign country today ... not sure I liked the feeling."*

What I found was God grabbing me by the collar and pulling me up to where I could smell his breath and saying something like this, *"Now do you see how insignificant you are? Can we now dispense with the sniveling over the disappointments and the fading inconveniences and learn a little something about thankfulness? Can we see that your life has been gifted with resources and blessings others in this world would kill—kill you, btw—to have?"*

[Journal Entry]—*"I realized looking out at the Indian Ocean that it was 20 years ago this month I first saw an ocean ... Now I've seen three ... made me consider how much time I've had at my disposal and wonder if I've made the best of it ... I wonder if I'll ever stop wondering that."*

[Journal Entry]—*"Being here, I am keenly aware of how pampered I am ... and how wasteful ... after being here, I wonder if wastefulness isn't a heartless ingratitude ... not everyone in poverty here is 'helpable,' but there are fine people who could use a break ... and they don't complain about it, they just live ... Had a conversation the other day with someone who wondered if these people could believe that God would supply all their need, as if He hadn't supplied it ... It's we who are inflated in our definition of 'need' ... but in all this I find a lesson on stewardship ... God has entrusted us with incredible riches, and that obligates us to*

*thankfulness, humility and even activity ... hopefully this lesson
only deepens, and I don't forget."*

What I found was not what I expected, which in a way was
what I expected. What I found was a beautiful country run in a
third-world manner ...

[Journal Entry]—*"Lots of trash for such a lovely place ...
Incredible sunsets, sugarcane fields, clunky trees with lacy leaves,
and gnarly trees with thick leaves, palm trees and a somewhat 'lush'
feel are all framed in litter, exhaust, and a society that seems busy
to do nothing.*

*"'Third world' was just a term to me before. Now it is
people: people and their problems, people and their diseases, people
and their addictions, people and their poverty. It was a lesson in
recognizing what you can do. I learned there is much more to it
than what I am doing."*

I learned there is even more to it than "preaching the
gospel" and calling it good.

[Journal Entry]—*"Futility comes to mind ... already it has
taken hold of my thinking. For all good intentions and prayers, will
much ever change in a place so captured by poverty? ... We came here
to share Christ; maybe I had hoped we would see numbers of people
moved by our initiative, but even so soon into this, it is apparent that
a trip by 15 Americans cannot overcome such huge obstacles, and
this place is so international, we're little more than a novelty, if that."*

We stayed at a converted rabbit farm which was
remodeled into a convention center and run by the Church of
England. They are wonderful in spirit and seemed enthusiastic
about our presence.

It was winter in South Africa, and the caretaker, Ian,
dressed for it. In spite of daytime temps in the 80s and evening
in the 50s to 60s, he was constantly wearing long underwear and
stocking caps.

The convention center was located outside Durban in a
lovely, tree-crowded countryside. Every morning we were looking

for animals and saw zebra and ostrich. There were avocado trees in the backyard; it felt exotic.

Just up the hill from where we stayed was an orphanage for AIDS children. All the kids in this place were HIV positive, and many were there because their parents had died of AIDS. In the middle of nowhere, it was still bounded by razor wire fences.

Overseen as well by the Church of England, the facilities were clean and neat and filled with kids between three and eight years old. In spite of the fact that many of the kids in this place will eventually die before their teens, the church makes sure they are as educated as if they lived in suburban Phoenix. Of everything experienced and thought, this was probably the seminal moment of the journey.

I would make the trip again just to be with these kids ...

[Journal Entry]—*"Went to the Lily of the Valley orphanage yesterday afternoon to put on a carnival ... You see things like this on TV, but when you go there, it is far more odd. With sixty or so little Africans running around laughing, eating, playing, simply being overjoyed at trinkets and cheap candy, strange sensations come to mind:*

"Cheapness ... in the sense of feeling guilty about taking personal pleasure from doing something so easily accomplished ... How good should I allow myself to feel throwing $12.50 worth of junk at kids abandoned and dying all for the sake of being able to say I did it?

"Shock ... A weird shock ... I felt like the richest man on earth ... I felt like I had incredible power ... power to make people happy ... African kids so taken by something so easily supplied: Crayons, candy, paper airplanes, and all of them so happy for it ... happier exponentially over what kids in the States would have been."

We ended singing kids' Bible songs. Surprisingly, they knew more than we did. I stood looking out at the setting sun and thinking of my home far away and wondering if I would ever be the same, somehow finally grasping where I was.

We walked home down the hill in the country to the sound of nothing but the shouts of the kids behind us and the stirring of dust beneath our feet. I don't know that I have ever felt so satisfied with something I have done. We sang a song on the way down.

The last lesson I learned came after being home, and it's sad. I discovered it only takes a couple months for some of the most important lessons in life to be forgotten. As I wrote about those orphans and our new impoverished friends this evening, I realized how little I think of them now, after such a short time.

It's the last sad lesson. I am here, and they are still there. Nothing has changed.

The High Cost of Living

When I was a boy, my grandpa lived not far from the mainline of the Chicago, Burlington & Quincy railroad in a forgotten Nebraska town. Almost hourly, the Burlington shot another freight past his house, barreling through Nebraska on its way to anywhere else. When my young ears picked up the faint whistle of an approaching train from miles away, I bolted through the kitchen, out the screen door, and raced across the backyard and gravel alley to the side of the tracks.

I stood there smiling, as if anticipating an approaching carnival.

As the train flew past, my knees weakened with the shaking ground. I was captivated by the bright colors of the rolling stock and deafening, piercing, shrill sound of steel on steel. I lingered there long after the caboose slid by me, taking in the wonder and smelling the hot steel and the dust of farms and listening as its rumble faded into the horizon.

Looking back over the last 15 years, I fight a sadness about what isn't coming back and a nagging sense I didn't stand by the tracks of my life long enough when it was passing before my eyes. Like a train bound for the Point of No Return, my daughters' childhood, my wife's bravery and trust, my son's arrival—my *life* feels as though it's fading over the horizon.

I went walking a few weeks ago; summoned might be a better word. That sense of sadness called me back to a familiar ribbon of sidewalk through what might be considered the lesser part of Bozeman. Cheryl and I walked this route countless times when we were younger and life was mysterious.

Before it became the past, our future was laid here. It seemed so easy then; it seemed elementary.

We talked about us and our kids and the church and about what we saw in the future. We wondered what we would build and if we'd survive. Along this sidewalk, we drew up plans for our future with the hope of dreams and unfettered by failures.

We pushed our daughters in strollers on this sidewalk and watched them play in Beal Park; we played with them. Along this path, we soaked up the welcome sun as spring chased away winter's gray, and we walked among the fire of late autumn leaves, pushing fallen ones with the shuffle of our feet. We welcomed seasons, relished our kids, and planned our future with the rest of our lives calling us onward.

When life calls onward, there is no real time for the now. It seems I looked up from those walks only to wonder what has happened with a decade and a half of my life, which grows shorter by the minute. When I'm still, I can feel the clock speeding up; where did the nineties go?

On this walk, I looked up to find myself looking back. As I did, a few things haunted me.

Weaving my way through the crowd of memories of me, I fear I have failed to appreciate that the good things and the simple moments I've preached to others were the most important ones. I remember promising myself I would appreciate my family, my wife, my talents, and my time, and all the irretrievable events of life.

Everyone's time streaks past them. We all put our heads down to carve out a life for ourselves and our loved ones only to look up and find twenty years missing. I can live with this as long as I know I lingered long enough to drain every bit of wonder and joy from what I've seen and experienced.

Some days, I sense I haven't.

Meandering along this sidewalk, I perceive some of the best of me is gone; it's a difficult thing to describe. I think the toll of fighting all the gack that comes packaged with life is catching up to me. Like high blood pressure, it's the "silent killer."

I've progressed from hearing it stalk me to wrangling for every desperate, innocent breath of happiness. For the first time, I know what it means to urgently desire God to place a heart of flesh in my chest where only a rock exists at the moment.

Retracing the path of my past, I thought of all Cheryl and I have been through, which is probably no more than you've been through. What becomes painfully clear on this afternoon, however, is the high cost of living. Idealism is dying, optimism is on life support, and I realized a few weeks ago that I don't care like I once did.

On this aged, washed-out gray concrete path I started to fully account for the cost of the accomplishments, survivals, and milestones of life we once dreamed of on this sidewalk. It isn't a cost that can be measured solely by time or scars or sacrifices. I see the sun leak from between flapping leaves of ancient maple trees, feel the receding warmth of summer in the clear sky above me, and I fear that the person walking here today has been emptied of the optimistic person who walked it a lifetime ago.

I lingered along those old tracks back in that drowsy Nebraska town many years past. After the trains disappeared from sight, I often crouched down and laid my hand on the rail, drawn by a strange thought. Those cold ribbons of steel reached back to where the train had been and reached out to where it was going; they stretched uninterrupted to the shores of two oceans. By touching them in Nebraska, somehow I felt connected to every state and every city along their path in both directions. I could get anywhere from there.

This walk felt like that. It felt as though, by walking the path of our past life, I was somehow connected to it and it called me to remember. As each step was placed down, I began to consider that often the only way to start appreciating what is happening now is to mourn having been careless about what isn't coming back.

Like sensing the rails connected me to where the train had been, the sidewalk connected me to who I was and compelled me to inventory who I had become. I discovered my life has cost me the best of me, but as long as I can lament what I am no more, I have hope of rebuilding it once again.

No one can avoid the high cost of living, but forcing ourselves to face those costs might just allow us an opportunity to recoup them. And that will be a life of wonder worth racing out to see and linger over.

....

CHAPTER 3

JOURNEYS & LEARNING

The Dragon Lady

She was an apparent contradiction.

Being a spry, older lady, she possessed the presence and confidence of a grizzled drill sergeant who had seen countless generations of fresh teenagers enter her art class. Her countenance was of a person who had weathered life, giving her a look of permanent scorn. The crevassed, leathery wrinkles on her face rarely gave way to a smile.

Listening to her, the sense she was continuously trolling for victims was unavoidable. She was looking for the naive and the foolish; "foolishly naive" would have been an instant kill. For me, this art class was an exercise in surviving the psycho-terror she dispensed with extreme prejudice.

In fact, the whole transition from Meadow Lane Elementary to Charles Culler Jr. High felt like graduating from Sesame Street to Cabrini Green. At least, that's how I felt about the whole thing, but I imagine it could be understood by anyone who has forced themselves to take one more step on the death march through junior high.

From kindergarten through high school, my kids attended a fairly small Christian school in a very tame city. When it was time for the eighth-graders to finally enter high school, the administration planned a chapel service so the current crop of senior high students could assure the incoming freshman that there was nothing to fear. They would be welcomed, not hazed.

The entire event was bizarre to me, chiefly because I couldn't imagine how anyone would be frightened to go to a Christian high school. It's like having an encounter session to calm kids' fears before moving up in Sunday school.

The step from Meadow Lane to Culler resembled the culture shock anyone would battle in a foreign culture. Personalities had to be learned and avoided, fights had to be dodged, merchants of cool had to be identified.

Walking the twenty blocks home after my first day, I was randomly selected to be someone's punching bag. There were any number of ways to be injured at Culler; most of them were unknown until you were on the ground gasping for air.

Every day at Chuck Culler Jr. High was another struggle at the bottom of the adolescent food chain.

I don't recall her name, but my 7th grade art teacher still prowls the hallway of my greatest fears. The dread I experienced every time I entered the room to undertake the challenge of transforming paints or clays into a thing of ugly is hard to describe, but it definitely exceeded that of the daily ceremonial beatings I tried to avoid.

The Dragon Lady's cold demand that we be conspicuously creative—or else—was the perfect, harrowing chaser to the onset of puberty. She caused ordinary American boys to contemplate running away from good homes, compelled by nothing more than the hope that in anyplace else, she wouldn't be there.

Which makes it somewhat ironic that one of the most enduring lessons of my life was forged in the fires of the self-contained hell of her art class.

It was in a sculpting assignment. We were to take ordinary, unappreciated items and craft them into something the Dragon Lady would consider to be art. Hearing the challenge, I remember feeling like the lone, drooling dullard in a room populated by creative geniuses, the kind of people who actually understand why Van Gogh cut off his ear. I felt doomed.

If that was an unfounded perception, my teacher did nothing to allay it when I handed her my sculpture. Being over twenty-five years ago, it is hard to recollect the exact conversation; my memory recalls it something like this:

Dragon Lady: *"What's this pile of waste?"*

Me: *"Ummm, my sculpture?"*

Dragon Lady: *"That's not a sculpture; it's the fruit of a mind that hasn't had an original thought since the Summer of Love."*

Me: *"Summer of Love?"*

Dragon Lady: *"Get this away from me. Go back and try thinking like a Homo sapien, like a creature to whom God might have given an opposable thumb for something more than sucking. Be creative. Think what you could do with these things besides the predictable, because if you bring anything like this back to me, I'll gut you."*

Me: [Staring blankly, feeling another pimple sprout on my forehead, and wondering if teenage runaway prostitution on the streets of Hollywood was really as bad as they said]

I think she was serious about gutting me. I know she was right about my sculpture. It looked like the self-expression of a person who considered gray "exotic." It was nothing more than differently shaped blocks of wood arranged and glued at peculiar angles atop a flat wood base.

The Freudian message behind my creation probably would have bumped me to the front of the line for anti-depressants. It made forensic accounting seem like an extreme sport.

I went back and summoned creativity. I did an end-around on my own predictability. Not because I was either particularly creative or suddenly unpredictable; she hadn't brought out the artist in me. It was more like she had brought out a survival instinct.

In an effort to shield what little dignity a thirteen-year-old possesses from a she-bear mauling, I went back to my ledge seeing my material in a new light. They were not merely art supplies; they were a riddle—a riddle I had to solve in order to live.

It wasn't shocking or earth-shattering. I threw it away the instant it was given back to me. My second sculpture was exactly like the first, only I had drilled a few holes in the base and in the blocks and inserted some wire between them, elevating a few of the pieces up off the surface. I made a second tier of blocks on top of the first in a similar manner.

This time, my project resembled something that might have been found in the wake of a freak tornado after it randomly threw objects together, impaling them with the speed of a super-collider. The sculpture before me could pass for modern art, without the art.

I didn't see her walk up behind me. Glancing over my shoulder, all she said was, *"That's better."*

That was enough. I exhaled for the first time in a week.

Looking back on the episode with the seasoning of maturity and age, with an acquired appreciation for applied creativity, I still hate her. I'm forty now, and she's probably dead, but she still scares me.

What I learned from this lady was not a lesson in creativity; she didn't help me get in touch with my innovative side or to "think outside the box." She taught me the value of someone who would say with the diplomacy of a flamethrower that I was thinking like a radish. It introduced me to the transformative power of "or else."

Like most people, I gravitate toward friends praising me from the stands or who nurse the wounds of my failures with soothing justifications. It's just hard to seek out those who hold you to expectations you are certain you'll never meet and who continuously warn you that life doesn't tolerate failures long. But, it's just as hard to endure a lifetime of stagnation.

Call it the value of an adversary or the power of discomfort. Whatever you call it, we all need a person who at times will scare us into exceeding our own predictability or releasing our stranglehold on security.

It seems to me we're all in some sort of food chain; I've found I rarely climb off the bottom without someone forcing me to believe in me.

Pity

I usually know nothing about catastrophe until I look out from the pot to see the natives shrieking and dancing in glee around the fire; it's a hazard of habitually believing the best about people.

Such was the case in a situation I was involved with early on in ministry that left an enduring pity in my spirit. And fear.

It happened between two men in this church over twenty years ago. At the time, I was the Youth Pastor, a husband of three years, and a dad for none; our church was also searching for a new Senior Pastor. Such searches bring people in congregations into closer contact than usual, often flushing to the surface brooding bitterness and angst that otherwise is left to simmer.

This "flush effect" is what fomented the showdown, as the two men involved had little love for each other and almost never spent much time together. One was a staff member serving as a roving missionary to rural communities and part time handyman at our church, while the other was a successful businessman.

When I walked into the meeting to discuss their animosity, I just didn't know how deep it was. I didn't know the sterile sanctification of one had targeted the other for elimination; I got a quick education.

Family is unspeakably important to anyone with a heart any more fleshy than the Tin Man's. There's a bugaboo with family as it relates to the ministry, however. It is that the Bible enjoins ministers to keep a tidy home.

Thankfully for me, not tidy as in clean or tasteful; if it hadn't been for Cheryl, I'd still be sitting on lawn furniture surrounded by posters, and my TV would be sitting on a shabby cinderblock entertainment center. By "tidy," I mean well-ordered. Pastors have been charged with maintaining a good marriage and well-behaved children who respect their parents.

This presents any number of hazards, as you can imagine.

I'm not begrudging the expectations, mind you; to the contrary, I embrace them. That does not mean, however, that I've not felt anxious at times about establishing what so many have found so elusive: a happy, healthy family. The fact that marital struggles and rebellious children could very well cost you your vocation represents a unique pressure point to ministry life.

Imagine that: Imagine at the point where your emotions have been most thoroughly pureed and intense stress has withheld sleep for nights on end and nothing makes sense anymore, you also are confronted with losing your employment. For good.

I've never heard of an engineer who was disqualified from engineering because his wife left him. I've not heard of a single case where an archaeologist was accused of being disqualified from digging in the dirt because her kid checked into rehab. No one in business, education, legal, medical, or any other profession faces this consequence for a marriage gone wrong or a child gone astray.

People in ministry do.

Sadly, a small number of Christians can't always be counted on to address the excruciating tragedy of family maladies in a minister's home with a proper mix of scripture and compassion. This is a disease usually limited only to those who think the Bible is a one-dimensional book of penalties and not a grace-soaked message to sinners.

I once walked with a man in the very early winter of his life who was extremely proud of his humility. He viewed the scripture as little more than a penal code to master for the humiliation of those less informed and the assessment of consequences to those ensnared in sin. As we walked, he told me that he believed if a pastor's child departed from the faith, even after decades into adulthood, not only should the dad/pastor resign, but the dad/pastor was almost certainly never called in the first place.

Of course, this man has never had children.

This is the ... stuff ... we live with. I learned a very long time ago to speak softly about other people's kids because mine weren't finished. But it's also because I know every person experiencing the daily dissolution of their marriage or the irremediable self-destruction of their kids takes time to offload their tears in private before ever braving the light of day, and I didn't want to thoughtlessly add to their burden.

Some of my comrades in ministry are veterans of this secret emotional purging. Inexcusably, as their life began to unravel, they were greeted only with the weaponized piety of the criminally spiritually smug. We all appear unaffected, don't we?

Which brings me back to the meeting.

Our staff member had a wayward son. I have nothing more to offer; we never spoke of it with real depth. I eventually concluded, however, that parents come to a place with their incorrigible children where the crushing sadness has turned an aching, bleeding, crying heart into a small rock. After that, they unplug themselves from what their kid is doing, almost as if it was no child of theirs at all.

Being an upper-middle-aged man in the ministry with a wayward adult child made this man vulnerable to the vicious sanctimony of the Upright Holiness Brigade. One of these was in the room that evening and believed that our staff member had forfeited the right to publicly teach the scripture because of his child's troubles.

I talk too much. Typically, I use fifteen words when six will do because I want to find the softest way to say the hardest things. And maybe I grew that way because I have watched fire-breathing inhumanity seem to look for feelings to char; untempered by self-awareness and humility, people turn on each other with visceral brutality.

I've watched spouses look each other in the eye and describe how they left their children home while cruising bars looking for someone to sleep with in retaliation for a spouse's cheat. I've had a person tell me they are leaving their mate and needed me to tell them because their spouse had no idea what was coming and there was no interest in reconciliation.

I've watched people desperately wanting reconciliation dozed over by another's unmitigated vengeance. I've seen faces melt as hardened, grown men sob like children because they don't know how to make their wife love them again while she sits empty and pitiless and completely unmoved by her first love's emotional breakdown.

In the Star Trek-The Next Generation episode "Skin of Evil," the ship's Security Officer, Tasha Yar, is killed by an oily, blackened blob who is the residue of all the anger and hatred and bile from a race of beings that dumped all their ugly emotions on him. Shed of those hindrances, they were free to be loving and kind to each other.

He just grew more and more vile and hateful.

After seeing the episode, I told Cheryl that is how I felt at times. People come into my office and are as ugly and punitive as their fallen nature cares to be and go home a little relieved for having done so. I just sit there after being dumped on, wondering how people get like that, and feeling a little piece of my humanity die.

Like I said, I talk too much.

The accuser of our staff member was one of those people who cared more about being right than about human beings—the letter of the law more than the spirit. And when he finally opened his mouth, there was nothing but criticism and accusation and denigration.

He didn't recognize our staff-member-handyman's ministerial commission given by this church. This business-man-church-member didn't understand why the staff member hadn't been dismissed a long time ago because of his glaring family issues. He loved him in Christ, naturally, but he had no respect for him whatsoever and couldn't fathom how any scripturally literate person could excuse his disqualification from ministerial office.

Me: [Blink, blink]

It was a tour de force of self-righteousness. He spoke with staggering prosecutorial conviction; had this church member been there, the Nuremberg trials would have wrapped up in about fifty-two minutes with the accused having swallowed their tongues in shame.

The staff member was a physically imposing person, but he was outgunned, many times over. To every indictment eloquently and confidently leveled by the business man, the staff handyman had only sentence snippets of retort.

He took it on the chin like all good ministers are supposed to do. At the heart of it all was a son.

To one of these men, this son was a loved and longed-for child. This was a boy he had prayed for, watched take a first step, say a first word, gave piggy-back rides to, taught to drive, and then watched throw their life and his love away.

To the other, he was a scourge, an embarrassment, and Exhibit A in the case against a man's calling. He pounded the point like a boxer landing blow after blow even after the nose has completely broken and blood flies on every punch. He was relentless, merciless, and mean.

To look at the staff member is to see a man who doesn't exude a need for pity. He was a "man's man." But I watched him that night with indescribable compassion and even pity. He didn't seem like a Reverend to me at that moment; he was a dad. And with every verbal haymaker, another layer of sadness was exhumed.

The beating ended when a friend called for compassion. Though such calls are always lost on spiritual attack dogs, a plea was made to understand matters aren't always as linear as we'd like them to be and sometimes mercy is the better part of justice.

My friend's words created only a temporary truce; the business man never relented in his crusade against the staff member, and his son never relented in breaking his heart. I pitied him; I still do. Yet, as the Lord seems to always manage, I discovered something from this thrashing that has endured for two decades.

The problem in our world is that small people, Christian or not, never stop seeking opportunities to aggrandize themselves on the misery of others. What insulates us all from such terror is not ridding the world of small people, but cherishing others and building lives that are immune to the thuggery of heartless individuals.

Even then, we're all too often helplessly reliant on the decisions of those we love to keep us from a beating.

Thank you, Baylee ... and Madison ... and Hayden ... and Cheryl for never providing a hollow-souled person the weaponry with which to bludgeon me. Thank you for not throwing your life nor my love away.

You are cherished, and you have kept me from the saddest variety of pity, the kind beckoned by heartache people never bring on themselves.

A Day in the Past Life

I was thinking a minute ago about something; it crept up on me for no discernible reason. It was a snapshot of a memory that seems so long ago.

Actually, to be more precise, it is a snapshot of two people on a day when they realized that life could exact unexpected nuisances and that faith could find unexpected blessings. Unfortunately, you don't realize those times have swelled up to meet you on the road of your life until they are ten or fifteen years behind.

I have grown to believe that the times in our past worth sitting back and smiling over are frequently experienced in the moment as trials. In fact, it seems that the greater those difficulties are, the greater the smile is when the snapshot is dragged out of the photo album in our memory.

I remember this couple in the infancy of a new life. Having just struck out on their own, they were still fumbling their way through the discovery of each other and living out the ideal of being "one flesh."

If money was tight, they would have considered themselves lavished in abundance; neither made more than minimum wage at meaningless jobs. But, they were in training. Having joined hands and made vows, they threw themselves at the calling to ministry by taking their first pit stop in Springfield, Missouri, to finish college.

Their one-room, cinderblock apartment in Springfield warehoused the eclectic essentials of a new marriage and nagging desire to have life lower the green flag. They were restless.

Springfield was a necessity because of the college but was never somewhere they would choose to live, so returning to their native Nebraska every chance they had refreshed their dreams in the company of family and friends. Each stolen weekend away prevented restlessness from turning to pointlessness.

The drive back to campus after such a stolen weekend always began on Highway 2 and wound through Nebraska City, perched above the banks of the Missouri River. Leaping over the Missouri on a bridge arched toward the sky for no apparent reason, Highway 2 landed on the other side of the watery border in Iowa.

On this glorious fall Sunday in 1990, only a few months removed from their wedding, their 1978 Honda Accord began straining to crest the bridge. Halfway up, it wheezed and gasped and then quit altogether. There was no choice but to let it coast backward to Nebraska where it finally rested lifelessly on the grass shoulder.

It was the first trial they faced together. They had no money for a tow nor to repair whatever was wrong, and they had no time. Springfield was 350 miles away where they were expected back for work and class on Monday morning. Certainly, life would throw much harder pitches at them in the future, but this minor league disaster would do until the big league ones arrived.

A quick trip across a milo field found a farmer on his way to town willing to drop them off at a mechanic's he knew. Together, they rode in the stranger's pick-up to a town that didn't know them to arrange for a repair they couldn't pay for.

These are the ingredients for life's best memories.

With tow arranged, the wheezing Accord was hauled into the garage. The mechanic saw the Montana plates and asked where we were heading. He was about sixty, gracious, and a genuinely interested man. He was also the kind of mechanic everyone hopes to find should they be broke and needing a car fixed in a strange town.

We told him we were on our way back to Bible college.

His quick return glance indicated he was taken aback. I don't know why, exactly, but he seemed surprised. I suppose in a sticky, rural Nebraska town this man had been raised in church. Playing the odds, I would guess Lutheran or maybe Catholic and, perhaps, he had never seen someone so young on the path of ministry.

He asked what denomination I was and what college I attended. As I answered, I could see him sizing me up as if comparing me to all the reverends who dispensed communion in his church over the years and fighting back disbelief. If they fit the stereotypical minister in my head, those reverends were all old when they showed up and simply older when they left.

Water in the gas, he diagnosed. It would take about an hour and a half to set right, just enough time to go for a walk and soak in a drowsy town seated on the edge of summer and dabbling its toes in fall.

We strolled beneath ancient elm and maple trees. People waved to us with a familiar two-finger salute raised wearily over their steering wheel. The concrete was gray and old, houses were sided in wood, storm windows were spotty but noticeable.

We talked, not about anything important; no major life decisions were made. Our marriage being only months old, our pause in a sidetrack village simply allowed us to step aside from the pace of life and enjoy each other's company in a way it seemed we hadn't since saying *"I do."*

Having no choice but to go nowhere, we took advantage of the chance to lazily rehash the hopes for our future that made being together so appealing. Walking seems to shake conversation loose, and this day began what has become a habit ensuring we talk with each other and not just to each other.

In my memory of it, we dreamt of a life that mattered and was free to enjoy blessings so often rushed over pursuing new ones. We dreamed the dreams of idealism and youth, unspoiled by failure or cynicism.

We also talked about how we couldn't afford this repair and wondered if we would get back to Springfield in time. There's nothing like uncertainty and worry to cast you clinging into the comfort of someone else's love for you.

The afternoon began blurring into early evening, and the call of locusts reminded us to return to the mechanic's shop for our car.

"No charge." He said, wiping his hands on the old shop rag. *"I don't charge men of the cloth."*

I never considered myself a "man of the cloth," primarily because I've never worn a ministerial collar. But also, because I was a twenty-four-year-old college student, it startled me. I felt like an impersonator.

He refused my offers to pay him with the only credit card we had, still in Cheryl's maiden name. He sent us down the road, complete with a full tank of waterless gas. We pulled back onto that bridge lunging across the Missouri River into Iowa, crested the peak with power to spare, and arrived in Springfield that evening.

Sometimes, I think, God afflicts our schedules and our abilities to *make* us take what so many hesitate to give themselves: Time. When He does, we have a chance to pull the curtain back and remember again the people we are, the people we hope to be, and the person we love.

In fact, I know now that afflictions are usually gateways to cherished moments, and the troubles we originally thought meant disaster become the home remedies we discover that preserve love in our lives.

Maybe the Lord knows it often takes a disaster to show us how right everything is.

The Could-Have-Beens

There was a tragedy in our town this last week. A man about 50 who used to own the Chevy dealership here was on the roof of a building and stepped on a piece of tin that wasn't secured. He fell about 20 feet onto concrete.

He was rich. He was in his prime. He was enjoying retirement. He was dead before he arrived at the hospital.

His death hit the entire community hard, because he was so visible and relatively young. You could see it on the faces of the people in church. They had the "wow, if it could happen to him, maybe it *could* happen to me" look on their face last Sunday. Which is where I took dutiful, homiletical advantage of the tragedy.

What better way to drive home the imminence of everyone's unknown date with death than an untimely, well-known one. My message was "Christmas Means a Chance." The overall idea was that Christ is the chance to reclaim what was lost in Eden. He's the chance we have for eternal life; He's the chance we have to change the world.

That chance is offered to people every week in church; most of those chances, on most Sundays, are easily and unfortunately dismissed. But this wasn't most Sundays, and I pressed on people not to let this chance brush by them like a stranger in a crowd.

I implored them to seize the opportunity to know Christ; it may be you, I warned, whose chest tightens as the last bits of cholesterol in your arteries seal off your heart from your blood. It may be you the next time that truck swerves into the wrong lane.

I know people don't like to hear it, and I don't like to say it, but that's life. Lives are made and ruined on ordinary days, days no one is expecting.

Consider this man, I said sensitively but boldly. The last thing on his mind on an ordinary Thursday morning was that he would be dead by nightfall. The thought never crossed his mind until he was falling the first few of twenty feet down to a concrete death.

Don't put off Christ, because the tragedies swim all around us like sharks; it's only by God's grace that we are not consumed with them. Don't wait for the last fall to try and settle accounts with God, because I can guarantee if you could spend 30 seconds with anyone—*anyone*—who let this chance slip by and then entered eternity, they would ask for only one thing: Another chance.

It went well. No one was saved, but people were moved. People were praying and sobbing. It was a powerful message, if I do say so myself, but the thing that made it so powerful was, unfortunately, the tragedy of one widely known man falling to his death and weaving shock into my sermon.

My son is nearly 4.

He is too cute for his own good and too graceless not to be a consistent source of belly laughs. He warms my heart with his gait, and in his presence, I'm usually grinning. He loves trucks, rockets, guns, and the Cornhuskers; he is generally everything I always thought my son would be, squared.

He has a window in his room beneath which is frozen dirt and rocks.

It is 15 feet in the air—only 5 insignificant feet short of the height that killed the local businessman 4 days ago.

Today, he fell out of it.

I got a call on my phone, and I was greeted with words that script the nightmares no one dares examine in the light of day: *"Steve? You better come home."*

It was my mom; she told me what had happened in a voice thinly veiling panic. As the world spun in my mind, I finally heard a cry in the background. He was alive, but his "tummy" hurt.

I met Cheryl and Hayden at the hospital. I couldn't believe how good he looked. Alert. Playful. He was scared to be in the hospital but, wonderfully, not so scared that he couldn't talk about bubblegum ice cream.

The doctor examined him and couldn't believe he was as well as he seemed. In fact, she found it so hard to believe she wanted to do a scan of his belly, saying something like this:

"Human beings just don't fall from those heights without getting hurt. In fact, when we get calls that kids fall from that height, we usually activate the trauma team."

We took him to radiology.

After twenty minutes of stiff, nervous casual talk with hospital types, the radiologist returned. I do remember these exact words, *"I just wanted to look at the miracle kid."*

If you could see the window he fell from, you'd know why the doctor said that, and you'd know why I think that is exactly what it was—a miracle. He plunged to the ground, landing in about the only place below his window without rocks and, apparently, on his butt.

So, tonight, he is sleeping soundly next to his mom, and I am still wired from all the "could-have-beens."

And that's the point, isn't it? The could-have-beens? What could have been today was an event that would have disintegrated my life and the history of my family forever. What could have been was a day that passes nightmare at the speed of light on its way to a darkness where words cannot go.

But it's not. It's just another Monday with a glitch.

In the aftermath, I do not know how parents survive the death of their children. My heart swells for them, and I am humbled by their unapproachable experience. I will pray for them with a little more urgency now. Neither do I know why God chose to spare us that dreadful experience, but He did.

I didn't get emotional until the doctors finally said he was OK and to take him home; it happened then. I walked into a bathroom, slid against a wall down to the floor and cried.

I wasn't weeping over the tragedy but for the grace. Simply overwhelmed by how much I didn't deserve to be spared the agony of the "could have beens," I sat there thanking the Lord between sobs.

After getting home, I held my son in my arms, almost afraid to let him go. Looking square into his eyes, I asked what

Happy Endings to Hard Days

happened. Spartacus replied: *"It was great, dad; I was just like Spiderman."*

I thought for a second and reminded him, *"Son, Spiderman doesn't hit the ground."*

In sparing my son, God spared me, and I was undone with humility and thankfulness. Thankful that God is Lord over the could-have-beens and, even more amazingly, the should-have-beens.

I also think the next time I speak of untimely deaths, I will speak a little more softly.

A Passport to Death

I hate sin because it sings a siren song, treacherously concealing the foulness of its intent. It stands on the street corners of our own desires, catching our idle minutes and our unguarded gaze, and reflecting them back at our own lust.

Her seduction calls us to relax on the tracks of life and deceives us into ignoring the oncoming train of consequence. She massages the throbbing pain of our responsibility with the oiled palms of procrastination, while we lay in the hospital of the damned.

We follow her down the darkened alleys of avarice and around the corners of conviction, slithering slowly to her poisoned paradise where all that matters is the moment. When we finally open our eyes, we understand an awful truth: She was our passport to death.

Sin is a merchant of evil packaged in beauty and distributes the addictive narcotics of neglect in the simple pills of pleasure. She's a whore of Satan whose only request for payment is the misery in the heart of one who wakes up face down in the gutter with the vomit of his own lust pooled around his ashen head.

From this toilet, you glance around, taking in sights of filth. Straining to pierce the perpetual darkness with reddened eyes, you see shadows of people slumped over in trash cans, crawling through refuse, pathetically trying to claw out of sewage.

You hear the mourning of a child whose dad never made it home, the wails of a mother whose family just split, the empty heaves of a baby boy with nothing left to throw up, the screams of a father who found his daughter lifeless with a needle in her arm, the hushed sobs of dreams lying dead beside the raped teenager, the deafening silence of an innocent wondering why the one he loves so much beats him so often.

It's her world: Death. In the dark of this day, death surrounds you; you have to run. You swear you will never go back, just like you swore last time. Coughing up the phlegm of a careless thought, you stumble.

Here, you find your house, your job, your family, your dreams, but they are different. The house is dark with an overgrowth of weeds; your family is there, only it is six feet below a cold headstone; you see your dreams, but they are oozing pus and being eaten by maggots.

It's too horrifying to be true ...

She was so beautiful. You never realized there would be a time you could never go back home, when you would be hopelessly stranded in sin's world. But in this world of death, you discover your prison too late and find yourself mercilessly sentenced to a lifetime remembering dreams of life.

Which is the other thing I hate intensely—Death.

I hate death because he is so blatant, riding unfettered across the landscape of humanity with a brutal efficiency. Sometimes he strikes with precision; sometimes his mark is off. Sometimes his victims leave behind a vault stacked full of decades; sometimes they live out excruciating years hoping for release that seems cruelly unwilling to arrive.

And the sucking voids of unsaid "I love you's" plague the footsteps of parents every fraction of a second the rest of their lives. The hollow whir of memories bouncing off abandoned dreams claw at the eardrums of families every milestone their loved one should have reached. The pleasant memories of little feet with big dreams evoke tears of all denominations all the days of a survivor's life.

Death dances around us every day. It dares us to see his empty face in the crowd, to hear the bony footsteps behind us, to sense his coldness across the street. He dares us to look around at life and see him in every moment of every ordinary day.

So we don't; we choose rather to ignore than acknowledge. And when we have ordered our world according to our desperate hope masquerading as confidence, death strikes a fatal blow to pretty little assumptions about life.

Frederick Von Schiller wrote that "truth lies in the abyss." Staring into the abyss carved out by death—and, seemingly, only then—we finally see the triviality of our priorities and the priority of our trivialities. The truth in this abyss dismantles our lives and mocks our choices and chides our neglect.

I hate it for reminding me that I am not engaged in a "career" but in an epic struggle to bring the exception of hope to a world ruled by despair. And I hate that sometimes only after someone is trapped in the world of death do they recognize sin for the beast she is.

In short, I hate it because everything James said about it in the Bible is true: *"Then, when lust hath conceived, it bringeth forth sin, and sin, when it is finished, bringeth forth death."*

For these reasons, I hate it all the more and take pleasure—*pleasure*, not comfort—from the promise of 1 Cor. 15:26: "The last enemy that shall be destroyed is death." I look to this day when, finally, the hatred will fade to victory beneath the glorious cross of Christ, as sin and death are consigned to their rightful place in a lake of fire.

The day cannot come too soon.

A Pleasant Exile

High on a plateau, in a place where footprints are foreign and pheasants call home, there is a stretch of land that divides the sky. On the right night, you can walk matted clumps of native grasses behind a regal English setter and be lulled to carelessness by the glow of the cragged, snow-dusted peaks of the Bob Marshall wilderness.

The subdued radiance of the setting sun simmers to a stew of weak yellows and falls out of the clouds, cascading over the towering granite mountains which guard "the Bob" from civilization. The sky seems to mingle with the peaks, giving birth to a new shade of brilliant, soothing purple.

Miles away from the pressure and deadlines left behind, you walk, thinking what a pleasant exile this is. Plodding through the lonely field, you feel guilty for not feeling guilty about feeling so good for doing nothing. Beyond the boundary of calendars, schedules, and responsibilities hounding you back in the city, a precious gift is discovered: peace.

A soft Canada breeze scrapes your cheek, whispering winter's approach. Ahead, a dog's tags ring as his nose bends around aging wheat and twisted alfalfa, following the sweet aroma of ringneck pheasant. He is your closest neighbor.

Alone. Here, there is nothing to plan, no issues to wade through, and your mind becomes lost in the rapture of having to think of only what it wants to.

The dog slows; he slithers with his shoulder blades pumping up and down like pistons. His belly is scraping the dirt, and his legs move slowly, deliberately. He is winding his way through the mangled nest of natural grasses and forgotten grain, following a scent no human nose could detect if it was buried beneath a rooster's wing.

He stops, rigid, but with glancing eyes ...

You walk up behind him slowly, talking to him like he actually understands English.

"There a bird here boy? ... Where is he? ... where's your bird?"

Putting your thumb on the shotgun's knurled safety, you brace yourself for the burst from the ground. After kicking the brush in front of his snout, you ready for the shot ...

Nothing.

"Go on. Find your bird ... where is he?"

He looks confused. He knows the bird should have been right there, and he seems disgusted that the rooster didn't have the courtesy to be in its proper place.

The dog slithers on through the tall, sparse wild oats. It's only a matter of time before his prey runs out of the field and the setter corners him between a rock and a double barrel.

You glance at the expanse of earth and recognize where you are. It's a place few people have trod, and you wonder why so many of them want to live in places where vacations are taken on asphalt or manicured grass.

A pair of whitetail deer stare at you from the next section. Their glare resembles people staring down an unwelcome neighbor spoiling the neighborhood.

The thoughts turn to the expanse. You feel small and comfortably obscure. For people who live under the tyranny of deadlines and constant connectedness, anonymity and obscurity are themselves a vacation; in this place, not only are you not known, there are no people to know you.

You look over the horizon. Seamless fields of golden grain stubble stretch for sections big enough to blanket entire counties in smaller states. They are peppered with spotty patches of brown, grainy grass; dirt roads slice through the patchwork of acres.

Six-wheeled grain trucks roll over those roads late into the afternoon, kicking up walls of dust that drift slowly out over the fields. Heading for busy grain elevators in tiny towns along the highline of northern Montana, these old Chevy one-tons in smeared colors race along as their rickety wooden racks restrain tons of wheat, just like they have for decades.

You feel a part of tradition. You feel connected to the earth, taking game from its bosom and witnessing the rush to bring in crops from the soil. In a world of shrink-wrapped dinners and granulated anything, the sound of dirt packing beneath your steps, the smell of harvest, and the taut feeling of dried blood on your hands reminds you that the world still turns on the bounty that God enables the earth to yield.

The experience is mesmerizing and the more you walk, the deeper into its wonder you're drawn. Feeling the connection to this tradition is as soothing as glowing windows in driving, drifting snowstorms and down comforters beneath drafty old window panes.

The cool wind taps your eye, and you blink, bringing you back to the business at hand. You notice the end of the field is only steps away, and your dog is slowing. He's more deliberate; he walks softly.

Stop.

His head jerks around like it was on a rope being yanked by something deep within the canopy of old weeds. Neck crooked, ears perked and nose wet, he looks determined, daring the bird to attempt escape.

His eyes refuse to move. His tail is flat as the horizon in front of you. He is so beautiful and so perfect, you almost forget that the last rooster of the day is breathing heavy beneath the magnificent nose of this royal canine.

As you walk up to where he has "set" the bird, your eyes glance one more time at the alabaster on the edge of the earth heaving to the heavens, beckoned by the dying embers of the sun's radiance. You know you shouldn't look at anything but the general vicinity of where that nose is pointed, but the vision is hypnotic and the experience is intoxicating.

Harvest. Light. Beauty. Bounty. Tradition.
PHLLLllllph!!!

A thunder of terrified wings erupts from a roof of matted grass. Cackles pierce the air and you fumble for the safety of the double barrel, startled at the proximity of the bird to your face. Raising the gun to your shoulder, you think, *"What a beautiful bird."*

It bolts straight up like a missile and slides to your left, turning its back to you, each beat of the powerful wings increasing its altitude and speed. You think, *"What a perfect night."*

You lay the cold wood of the Weatherby to your cheek and put the bead sight just beneath the ring of the neck. Squeeze the trigger.

Wings beat harder and faster.

One shot left.

Put the bead on the shoulder of the bird. Squeeze the trigger. The gun pushes your shoulder sharply back ...

The fading sound of relieved wings pumping the air and gliding down into a gentle coulee paved with prairie grass is the only sound that disturbs the settling heaviness of nightfall. You stand there watching, not thinking so much of what you did wrong to miss, but of what a wonder it was to even be there.

Your dog looks at you with an expression that says, *"Seriously?"*

He'll get over it.

Walk slowly back to the truck worn out but ready for a pork sandwich at the diner down in the tiny town nestled among an oasis of cottonwood trees. Their thick trunks line the streets and drop giant leaves on old streets. A smooth, lazy stream meanders through town.

Before driving there, you pour water into a bowl for the dog and lean against the old orange Suburban.

On the top of a plateau, where footprints are foreign and pheasants call home, you gaze out across the shimmering stubble field into a vast expanse of nothing. The wind is whistling though the power lines strung between short weathered poles and lulling the earth to sleep. The sun is pouring its final light from the heavens as it turns the watch over to the stars.

The silence is deafening. The loneliness is exquisite, and the memories priceless.

Dinner waits down below.

Death Rattle

Every "first" is memorable—first fight, first fish, first kiss, first audit. Firsts are almost as memorable as lasts.

I experienced a lot of "firsts" in the initial years of ministry. I've noticed lives go on and needs arise despite whatever calamity has monopolized our energy or what inexperience or incompetence we hope will excuse us from life's complications.

Before I was pastor of the church I currently serve, I was an assistant caught up in a congregation's search for a new pastor. As the process began, all duties that would normally land on the actual pastor's desk were forwarded to me, no matter how unprepared I was and despite the fact I had no desk. During this interim time between pastors, I officiated at my first wedding ceremony and my first funeral.

I actually had two weddings before I was called as pastor here. Neither of them comes to mind without risking seizures. They are the chief reasons I often say I'd rather do a funeral than a wedding. Any day.

I also had two funerals before settling into the pastorate. The first occurring only a couple months into the search and while the first candidate was in town considering the position. I've noticed death is never convenient.

The funeral was for a man with a good history in our church. He was older and had married a younger woman; together, they had a very young son. An imposing man in his health, his gentle spirit was always evident in his speech.

Around the time the pastor I worked for was departing, this man's prostate cancer returned. Not only had I never done a funeral, I had never danced with hospice.

When it became clear this was the last relapse of his life, he was placed in a rest home facility oddly located in an older neighborhood of town. I visited him there a couple times a week and dreaded each one.

It was the kind of facility that had an overwhelming stench of dying and sorrow. The smell assaulted my emotions like a mustard gas for hope; the sights frightened anyone who was sane. The Gentle Giant was warehoused in a room that could not possibly be any farther away from the entrance.

I still remember the gauntlet I had to walk to get there: Through the front door, take the stairs down on the left, turn left and walk an eternal hall, then make a right and head for the metal emergency exit at the end of the cinder block tunnel, last door on the left. Along the way, try not to make eye contact with the discarded humans scattered aimlessly in the hall drooling in wheelchairs, try to ignore the screams from dark rooms and the passes made by old women in hospital gowns thinking they were twenty-five.

I am not trying to be unkind—honestly. The carnival of misery I waded through to visit this man made me rethink my understanding of medical ethics.

In his room, it was always a little brighter. The Gentle Giant greeted me with a smile each time; there was a little daylight window above his bed that let precious sunshine into the pervasive darkness.

He was diminished; in the end, cancer eats people.

I would sit for a while, and we'd talk; he'd share some scripture he was reading, and I'd pray. I wasn't the pastor, but I don't think he cared; human warmth needs no ordination to be appreciated.

His wife was there only once when I was. She was scared and wore the fright on her face like a giant scar. His room was a cinderblock cavern with ancient linoleum squares on the floor; only curtains separated the other, unoccupied beds from his.

I sat in the plastic chair next to the bed while she stroked his hair and told me he was getting better. She was force feeding him the latest non-traditional cure for cancer: Algae. But not just algae, "Super Blue-Green Algae" from Klamath Falls, Oregon. Accept no imitations.

Of course, Super Blue-Green Algae from Klamath Falls, Oregon was also super expensive.

There was a time in our church when this Super Blue-Green Algae commanded more devotion from people than Jesus did, and devotees displayed greater evangelistic zeal for converting people to its magical healing powers than to the Gospel. Visitors to church were sometimes eagerly invited over to members' homes, something I interpreted as caring for souls.

Turns out, the hospitality was extended to pitch algae, not share Christ. There were people who never returned to our church because of this appalling hypocrisy that would make a money-changer blush.

I even had a cassette arrive in the mail from someone writing like I should know who he was, asking me a simple question: Did I know why the Bible said Moses' strength never left him nor his sight grew dim?

The first thought to come to mind was God. Naturally, that was incorrect. Moses never suffered standard human deterioration because—yes, I'm serious—he ate algae.

At the time, we had a woman in church afflicted with severe psychotic episodes kept reasonably in control by medication. One of the Super Blue-Green Algae enthusiasts took me and Cheryl out to dinner and informed us that Super Blue-Green Algae from Klamath Falls would cure this woman, and they wanted to take her off the prescriptions and replace them with the wonder fungus from Oregon (I know algae is not a fungus).

Oh. And they wanted the church to pay for the Super Expensive Super Blue-Green Algae.

I suggested I might be open to it if *they* paid for it and they were willing to take this woman into their home should she again be found wandering the streets naked, mumbling about demons she saw at Walmart.

They never brought it up again.

But I was biased by then. I learned a couple years earlier to hate—*despise*—modern witchdoctors who prey on hope. The lesson came while sitting on that hard plastic chair watching a terrified widow-to-be place the entire faith for her husband's recovery in capsules of pond scum.

She told me stories of people on death's door raised up to new vigor. She told me how the medical "establishment" didn't want people to know the healing powers of nature in general and of Super Blue-Green Algae from Klamath Falls, Oregon, in particular. She could see him getting better; they were going to beat this thing and get back to life.

I smiled and nodded.

As she spoke, he gazed up at her face, taking it in like a tonic running low. He wasn't listening to her predictions of victory, and her manufactured confidence that he would soon be home was met with a look that tried to silently capture her every subtle beauty as though it could be his last chance.

I hated the person who told her these pills would give her husband back to her. Hated.

She looked back at him and gave him a playful charge to keep popping the algae on schedule. She made him promise to do so twice and then she left.

The Gentle Giant watched her leave, pausing a couple seconds after she disappeared into the tunnel to make sure she was gone. He looked at me with a knowing smile.

"She thinks I'm leaving here."

"Yes, she does."

"I'm not."

"I know," I replied softly.

He nodded at me. It was the first time we had openly admitted it. He then took the occasion to tell me something I didn't know how to handle.

"I'm scared." He looked up at the ceiling.

I didn't know what to say. Christians aren't supposed to be scared of death, I was told. We have an assurance of eternal life through the sacrifice and resurrection of Christ; death is just life by other means.

"Why?" It burped out of my mouth without warning.

"I'm scared to meet the Lord. I'm scared he'll punish me for my sins."

Uncharted territory is a gross understatement about where I was at that moment in this conversation; I was literally speechless. No class in Bible college covered this. It is impossible to express how inconsistent his fear was with Christian theology and orthodoxy.

The abstract comfort theology and orthodoxy provide in days of endless health sometimes withers when death begins to have definable features.

"You don't know how I've lived, what I've done."

He was right. I only knew a snapshot of his life, which is the extent to which most of us know each other.

I've learned that people frequently walk into our lives all cleaned up from the mess and sorrow and mistakes and damage that we accumulate from living. To me, this Gentle Giant was a sweet-tempered, godly man who loved the Lord and His people— and had all his life.

But he knew himself better. He knew how lamentable the missteps had been, how intentional his sins were. Ironically, because he knew his fear wasn't Biblical, it was inconsolable and intractable.

I tried to comfort him with the promises of the Word of God: *"Precious in the sight of the Lord is the death of saints." "I go and prepare a place for you, and if I go and prepare a place for you, I will come again and receive you unto myself that, where I am, you may be also."*

He listened with a smile. I knew the words bounced off the hardened armor of fear.

He only lasted a couple more visits. Toward the end, he told me his wife had doubled then tripled his intake of the algae, and he was concerned over how much money she was spending on it. But if it gave her comfort, he'd oblige.

I went in the last afternoon and thought he was sleeping. When his head turned to me, there was no smile, no hope left. The time had come to put affairs in order. He gave me a couple of instructions for his funeral. He picked the hymns he wanted sung, and he handed me his massive Bible to preach from so that the book in which he found life would also send him off into death.

I assured him everything would be followed to the letter, prayed, and told him I'd see him soon. He was wheezing now but managed a shallow smile before turning his head away.

The call to come to the rest home came about 9 pm a few days later. It was a short drive from our apartment, and I was led to a different room he now occupied. His wife was there; she had a look of frantic emptiness.

The room was intentionally dark with only an eerie glow from dimmed lights slicing through the presence of death. This man was now completely withered away. His large frame was barely skeletal, and his face was elongated with his mouth wide open; he looked like a Picasso painting.

I was devastated at how much he had changed since my last visit with him. Cancer had double-timed its savagery, and the person before me was irreconcilable with the man I knew from church.

And then the night was pierced with a terrifying scream.

The morphine drip was wide-open, dumping pain killer into his vein like a garden hose. Even with enough narcotic in his body to kill an entire herd of buffalo, he unexpectedly bolted straight up, eyes wide open, and screamed at the darkness.

His wife moved to calm him; his body collapsed onto the gurney. As she gently repeated, *"shhh ... shhhh,"* I could hear his breath gurgle.

The "death rattle" was here.

It rattled *me* to the core. I stood motionless, scared to even blink. His breaths were fewer and fewer, slower and slower.

And then another round of screams, only this time, he screamed at someone, someone no one could see. My memory recalls his words, but I don't trust it. What I remember his saying is too disturbing to be mistaken about, although Cheryl assures me my distress was evident and she remembers it to this day.

This isn't the way I was told Christians die. I was told there was peace—and tender assurances given to family of a certain reunion. I was expecting inspiration and a wonderful story of a Believer gliding from life's shores into the glory of his Lord.

This was something else ... there isn't a word for it.

On the day of the funeral, the church was full. I planned out the service to the last detail, having consulted everyone I could about how to do a proper funeral.

We sang each song he requested, and I used the titles of the hymns as points in the message I preached from his Bible. With his casket before me, I told everyone of how a detestable disease had stolen this Gentle Giant's vitality, but now—at this very moment—he was with His Lord.

In meeting Christ, he was finally freed from the ruthless tyranny and torment of cancer. It was a good funeral, especially for a first one.

I never mentioned his fear. I never spoke of his terror as he slipped out of time and into eternity. I have never forgotten nor ceased to be disturbed by either of them.

I don't know why the Gentle Giant passed so traumatically. I have hoped it was merely the explosion of emotions and morphine colliding and that he has been enjoying the company of Christ for the past twenty years. But what I witnessed made me think that people frequently speak too cavalierly about grave matters. There are things we have tamed in our imaginations that remain wild and savage and on the prowl out those doors, down that road.

Far from shaking my faith, this death helped me to recognize that life is serious business and that impetuous indulgences can sometimes dog us to the very end, even when they have been expiated on the cross of Christ. In the end, we simply can't outrun our own conscience; it catches up to all of us.

The experience compelled me to frame my life around what matters most. Solomon said it best when he wrote that it is better to go to a funeral than a party—unconventional wisdom, to say the least. His point being that, by beholding the end we all face, our lives can be better today.

My first funeral is testimony to that truth. In an unexpected way, I'm grateful to have heard the death rattle and watched as the grave enveloped this man, because it made me understand how the end reveals everything and taught me a lesson learned no other way than up close. And scared.

It is a lesson on regret. I walked away that grim evening knowing the one thing I didn't want to regret when I died was how I lived.

....

CHAPTER 4

ELEGY & FAITH

A Different Kind of Groupie

I've never considered myself a writer.

I always figured that in order to be a writer, I had to have vast amounts of experience from exotic adventures tainted by sea air. I believed it necessary to be a little more twisted than I actually am, that I required some deep sense of angst or brooding—an addiction would be helpful.

There are only two things in my life that I believe qualify me to be some sort of a writer. The first is cynicism. Cynicism always keeps you from taking yourself too seriously and ensures that you are the hardest and cruelest critic of your work.

Truth is, however, I really never intended anything I typed to be taken so seriously as to be critiqued. Honestly. Many writers dream of being writers; I dreamed of fishing. Writing sounded like work.

The other qualification is compulsion. I don't really know how to explain this, except to say that when something happens in my life or a memory is summoned or a milestone passed or any number of other things, I'm often compelled to put it on paper.

In his book, "Lake Wobegon Days," Garrison Keillor tells of a college class that is interviewing a famous writer. One student raises her hand and asks, "Where do you get your ideas for writing?"

The writer responds, *"I guess I could say I get my ideas for writing from writing, but that would beg the question, wouldn't it?"*

Maybe. But it's also true. Sometimes I sit down and start writing, not really knowing why, and soon there is actually something to read.

I vaguely remember a high school English teacher marching me into her office; I don't remember the reason why. I *do* remember that on the way in, one of my former English teachers looked up and noticed us. The one leading me through their mysterious teacher-lair glanced at the other and said I'd be convinced my future was in English by the time she finished with me that semester.

The other one replied, *"I hope you have better luck than I did."*

I was a little amazed. I hadn't realized either one of them intended to convince me of anything other than actually coming to class.

Even if I had known their intentions, however, I would have dismissed them with the terror that accompanies swatting a wasp off my arm. A *future* in English sounds a little like saying someone has a future in Elizabethan Poetry. They are both gentle ways of saying you have a future in obscurity and poverty.

And English teachers are the people students look at with pity, the way a successful tycoon might look at a street person and silently wonder, *"How did he wind up like that?"*

That's the constant wonder surrounding English teachers: *"What did you do to God that He would sentence you to a lifetime of English?"*

To me, that wasn't much of a future.

Additionally—and this was probably more of an obstacle for me—I hated English. I don't even remember high school English. Really.

I wanted to be good at science or politics. English was for old women and bookworms; I considered myself neither.

Consequently, any "future" I would have enjoyed in English was sacrificed for a "present" in bass fishing.

But it's funny how things go; it's funny who was right and who was wrong. I hate to admit to anyone that I enjoy English in the same way I'd keep pretty quiet about my enjoyment of "Say Yes to the Dress."

If I did enjoy it. Which I don't.

Seriously. Never seen it.

This English confession is the fruit of some reflection and a generous act of kindness.

I learned much at my alma mater, Baptist Bible College, more than I realize, I suppose. But I really didn't like it there much. This tends to make me the odd man out when in the company of fellow alums who go beyond "waxing" to encrusting themselves in nostalgia for their college days.

From their memories come countless stories of professors. Many of these tales involve a beloved ecclesiastical icon who consumed class time spinning yarns of yesteryear's gallantry instead of assigning work. Remembrances of taxing doctrinal exams from demanding teachers and warm memories of pastoral professors dispensing sage advice like a vending machine are told and retold every time graduates assemble.

What I never—and I mean, never—hear are stories or warm recollections about the professors who have kept us all from looking like drooling St. Bernards while expressing our homiletical insights in public. It wasn't the faithful college president who taught us when to employ "me" instead of "I." It wasn't the veteran pastor with proverbs up his sleeve who demanded we write (and therefore, think) in complete sentences; no icon ever cared if we read a book that had nothing to do with the Bible.

This is the lonely domain of the English professors. When I do hear stories of them, it's like watching a person recount the Bataan Death March or a day in The Killing Fields. Their eyes glaze over and look at something far away. They are no longer in your presence as they glance around the English classroom in their memory ... they speak with reservation ...

"It was awful. I ... I can't really begin to describe ... I don't like to talk about my experiences much ... But it was just horrifying. Participles, infinitives, subjectives, and objectives ... you wouldn't believe it if I told you. Everywhere in this place was the smell of sweat and the whimpering of the vanquished. Only the strongest survived ... and even most of them fell under the blade of Shakespeare. I never realized Bible college could be so ... I didn't go to Bible college for English, bless God, I only wanted to preach ...Thank God it's over; my therapy has helped, but my battles in the trenches of English will ... haunt me the rest of my life. I only pray God spares my children from it."

English is the torpedo that sinks the SS "Babdist," the fly in the Fundamentalist ointment. Correct English is the bane of old-time, old-fashioned gospel preachers everywhere.

This, I think, is why warm paeans of English professors are never shared by alums at casual reunions. Let's face it: you hated them. Not in the *"hating the English, loving the professor"* way; you hated them in the*"I really hate you"* way.

They were your messengers from Satan, sent to buffet your flesh.

I never got to know any of the theology professors during my time in college. For one thing, they usually had a pack of yapping fanboys surrounding them like groupies fawning over rock stars. Staying as far away from those people as geography would allow always came naturally to me; consequently, I never spent much quality time with Bible professors.

However, there was plenty of room around English teachers, not that I was a fanboy myself. I'd be surprised if any of them knew who I was five minutes after I left the classroom, but it was easier for me to like them because they seemed normal, in an English sort of way.

I don't think it's an exaggeration to say I learned more from them than the Bible professors—both in terms of quantity and usability. English professors seemed to work very hard and treated their subject with as much urgency in Bible college as the Bible professors treated theirs.

As far as I could tell, they did all this in the utter absence of anyone reciprocating their urgency. This perception was confirmed to me not long ago when a meaningless email I shared on a pastors' discussion list was forwarded to my last English professor in college.

I simply wrote how much I appreciated this unappreciated culture of instructors after someone asked a general question about who our favorite college professors were. A couple weeks later a card found its way to my mailbox.

The return address was in Springfield, Missouri, from Mary Boschen. Which is strange to type, because I still can't get myself to be so familiar with my professors as to call them by their first name; they will always be "Mr." or "Mrs." to me.

She was complimentary not only about what I wrote but, most importantly to an English teacher, how I had written it. Her words were kind and gracious, and she actually remembered me. Like getting a good grade delivered a decade late, her card was unspeakably thoughtful and meant as much to me as a Bible professor's compliment would mean to a fanboy.

So, for all the lonely professors who have thanklessly done so much to halt the perception that butchering the English language is a Baptist distinctive, I would like to say thank you. Thank you on behalf of all your students who were terrorized and tormented by your medicinal curriculum, whether they were enrolled in Bible college or an Ivy League university.

What you did not receive in appreciation from your former students, you now have in gratitude from your graduates, with interest.

And goodnight, Mrs. Boschen, wherever you are.

Goodbye, Jim

I "remembered Jim" a few stories back after seeing a picture of our 20th high school reunion. Almost three years to the day I did, Jim suffered a heart attack in his doorway; he was dead before he hit the floor.

There seem to be times when life ushers us into circumstances every one of us thinks are too absurd to actually happen. Until they do. That absurdity invaded my world when I was asked to give a eulogy for my first best friend's funeral.

This is what I said:

I know that many here don't know who I am or why I am speaking this morning. My name is Steve Van Winkle; I grew up in Lincoln; I graduated from East High; I have a wonderful wife and three unbelievable children; I pastor a church in Montana ... and, once upon a time, Jim Crew and I were best friends—brothers, I suppose, is a better word. For six years, we were inseparable.

Like everyone here, I have had an emotional week, a week of looking back. The scripture says that in the day of prosperity, rejoice ... but in the day of adversity, consider ... I have considered much the last seven days.

I would like to share some of those considerations with you this morning.

I have so much to be grateful for in life. God has given me many blessings of which I am not worthy. My thoughts this last week helped me understand that I received one of His greatest blessings in 1978, when my entire life was at the height of vulnerability.

Twenty-nine years ago my dad had recently departed, but God showed His care for me with a most unappreciated gift: He gave me a friend. As two refugees from the nuclear family, my friendship with Jim turned out to be the seminal event of my childhood.

So this morning, I guess I am the voice of the past—of the best past. I was there when Jim wasn't "Mr. Crew," when he wasn't "dad," when he neither held degrees nor was "chair" of anything.

I am the voice of when he was just Jim—our friend, our brother, our student, our son. And his own very unique person.

Whether it was his sarcasm, a well-timed gesture, or just an unorthodox approach to a situation, no one ever made me laugh like Jim. I think Jim laughed so much because he had to laugh so young. He had to laugh out loud or cry alone, and we were just laughing with him.

Laughter is what he would have wanted today.

But this morning it's also my obligation to honor him, to acknowledge all he meant to me, all he means to me, all he means to all of us.

Tears are hard, but they are a good thing this morning. Tears tell the world that the life you celebrate did more than live; they testify to a life that gave, that mattered.

And this is how Jim's life mattered in mine. Let me tell you about my friend this morning and see if we have the same kinds of memories ...

Jim was a friend who pushed me ...

Jim had a way of taking the lead into the places that timid teenagers fear to tread. He was the guy who got me out of my house so I could often get into trouble. But it was great trouble. Fun trouble. I paid for it sometimes, but it was worth every grounded day.

Jim shared my first arrest. Having adjoining paper routes early Sunday mornings, we often slept over at each other's house Saturday night. We usually took these occasions to sneak out into the night and had made a cottage industry of tp-ing houses. In fact, there may be some people here whose house fell victim to that spree (I'm sorry).

Our vandalism ended in the wee hours of a cold December night while walking along 70th street when a police car whipped into the driveway in front of us. Noticing a couple of teenagers cradling grocery sacks in their arms at an unusual hour, the officers suspected mischief, blocked the sidewalk with their vehicle and told us to get into the car.

Jim politely declined; however, the officers prevailed with a stern voice indicating this wasn't an invitation. Once inside, they asked us what was in the bag.

Jim answered, *"Eggs, toilet paper, and shaving cream,"* as casually as if he was just asked his shoe size.

"What are you doing with that at 2:00 am?" the officer asked.

"Our dad sent us out to get it." I believe Jim expected the officer to buy that. His belief in this lie was breathtaking, and I admired his feigned conviction.

They then asked where we lived. I—being just beyond terrified—dutifully gave my information. Jim, on the other hand, remade himself into a guy named "Joe Todd" whose address seemed to be that of a friend's house across town and whose parents could be reached at this friend's phone number.

Jim had lied to the police, and they would never know otherwise; he was going to escape and I was going to juvie. I wished I had thought of that ... right up until we were told they were taking us home.

This is my mom's favorite Jim story. She wasn't laughing so much back then and grounded me for a month; I served every single day of that judgment.

Jim got me arrested when I was 13, and I love him for it. Jim pushed me to do things I was never motivated to do myself. And they were things that went beyond trouble, things like school, sports, girls, friends.

Jim Crew was my best friend in 1978, and he pushed me to rise above my own predictability like no one else in my life ever has. He pushed me to see the humor in life. He pushed me to see the value in an education. He pushed me to think for myself. In the years when so much of life is laid out, Jim pushed me toward the person I am today.

Jim was also a friend who stood side by side with me ...

When we were in jr. high, we usually walked to school, and Jim always carried a radio with him. Some mornings, however, riding the bus was necessary, but it didn't stop Jim from playing that stupid radio obnoxiously loud.

One such morning in 7th grade, the driver told him to shut it off. Jim told him—in Jim's special way—that he saw no need to do any such thing. Jim got kicked off the bus, so I got off with him.

I can see it like it was yesterday. As the bus pulled away, Jim stood on the curb like the mouse in those "last great act of defiance" cartoons, casually waving to the driver with a single finger. I just looked at him, speechless at how he just gave an adult the Jersey salute; we were dead.

Standing by ourselves at the bus stop the following day, we watched the bus come up slowly. As it did, we noticed the driver was the same guy who kicked Jim off the day before. He slowed down and slowed down and when he was just in front of us, he leaned forward in his seat and pressed his own finger on the glass ... and drove off.

And there we stood, staring at each other with equal parts disbelief and elation. Disbelief because we had never seen a grown up act like a child, and elation knowing this guy had given us at *least* a half day off of school, maybe a full day if we played our cards right.

But there was Jim. The first time an adult flipped me off, there he was. I loved that—admired that—about him. To my passivity and diplomacy, Jim was a flame-thrower who took nothing from no one.

In the years when boys struggle to become men, neither of us had one to look to. Yet, I could look over and see Jim, and Jim was always there.

To this day, as God as my witness, I hear his voice when I have to confront someone, or when I meet people, or when I make people laugh. The notion isn't as sharp as it once was, but when I am forced out of my own comfort zone in my job or in life, somehow, in some language I recognize from my teen years, I ask myself, *"What would Jim do here?"* or conclude, *"This is how Jim would have done it."*

Because that's what he did. He took people and showed them what *could* be. He was always learning, acquiring knowledge, genuinely interested in things. Jim was naturally inquisitive without sounding disingenuous. He showed me I could know people better with a few more questions; I could enjoy life more with a few more hours out of the house; I could go farther with a little more thought.

Wherever I was, whatever faced me, when I was down for the count, my best friend was always there. When I felt like giving up or laying down, Jim kicked me in my comfort, and we moved on.

Jim was a friend who kept me looking ahead ...

Has any friend ever known you like the best friend you had when transparency was natural and not dangerous? Has anyone ever known you beneath the fronts we project like the best friend you had when the days stretched long before you and the sun shone without end?

I was the friend Jim had when we both talked about life with innocent optimism, when we made plans for our futures without the whiff of cynicism. Twenty or twenty-five years ago, he told me about all the people in this room this morning.

I took some time to read the comments left on the obit website. I have read notes from students and from colleagues and from family. I know so few of the names that have shared their grief or revealed their favorite moments or expressed their loss, but I heard of you years ago.

None of you know it, but when we were boys, like all friends, Jim talked about what he wanted his life to be. And when he did, his family was there.

When I was a kid and Jim was my best friend, his family filled his worries. I suppose that's because when his home was void of the man-of-the-house, Jim filled the opening at an age earlier than anyone should have had to. His family touched him in ways he probably wouldn't have wanted them to know.

The students of his and the colleagues here today: I heard of you 20 years ago as well. One thing about Jim I will never cease to admire and which profoundly affected me was that he knew himself so well.

As early as 15, 16, or 17, when we were kids in jr. high and high school, I couldn't wait to leave Lincoln; I wanted nothing more than to move to the mountains. Jim, on the other hand, couldn't wait to start a life here, as a math teacher, at East High.

Looking at you this morning, it's clear that Jim's life stands as testimony to his self-made courage that looked dreams in the eye and dared them not to come true. You should all know this morning that you represent what Jim would have called a dream come true.

And his daughters: I want you to know how you affected your dad. I can't remember a time when he and I dreamt about our future when he wouldn't say he didn't want ANY kids. Every time I asked him why, he said he was afraid they'd be like him.

Your dad consistently rejected the notion of ever having children when he and I were kids ourselves.

Then you girls came into his life, and I never saw a man so in love with his daughters and so captivated by being a dad. I can't express how much your dad didn't want kids until he had you; you girls came into his life and showed him how incomplete he was. Not so long ago, your dad told me how he could never imagine life without you and how indescribable his love is for you.

I look around and I can assure you that this room, this morning, represents all Jim ever wanted from his life. When we were kids, I often watched him walk right up to the ledge of a decision or a choice that would have compromised everything and everyone here today.

And then I watched him turn around. It was like he saw this day, like he saw all of *you*, and refused to jeopardize this moment.

I guess I'm here this morning not because I know Jim the best nor because I have spent a great deal of time with him over the last decade. I'm here because I was Jim's friend when his life was under construction, when he was building toward the impact he would have on every life here this morning.

I come here today to give witness that when I was a kid, Jim saw you all. Jim was moved by you all, and Jim dedicated his life to working with you and teaching you and raising you and protecting you. He did it long before some of you were born and before some of you knew who he was. He spoke of it, dreamed of it, pursued it—and your presence here this morning proves it.

It proves that an ordinary kid, dispossessed of the advantages so many take for granted and against most odds, can dream worthy dreams and die knowing they have become his life.

Gimbal Lock

High school, for me, was merely an obstacle to my fishing and hunting. This meant I spent a great deal of time calculating exactly how much I *didn't* have to attend class and how many assignments I *didn't* have to do in order to skip then and still graduate later.

The time I stole from my education was invested on farm ponds, leisurely mornings, and some hunting when it snowed. Or when the season opened. Or when it was about over. Or when I had shells.

It was a risky venture. My vice principal, "Doc," put an end to it when he intercepted me leaving school to take a long lunch at the expense of Spanish class. With three weeks left in my senior year, he took me into his office and starting filling out my expulsion papers before my very eyes.

At that moment it hit me that I was a poor man's Ferris Buehler, and I basically begged him, on my knees, to put the pen down before someone got hurt (namely, me). Mercifully, he did.

But the casualties were there. I failed Spanish and Weight Training. How does a person fail Weight Training, you ask? By having it be the first class of the day at 0-dark-thirty when I usually preferred to rise at the crack of eleven.

I passed my other classes, but I still don't know why or how. As God is my witness, I never turned in a single homework assignment my entire three years at Lincoln East High School. Not even in Physics, where the final project was an unholy percentage of the final grade.

I took Physics because it sounded like something I should know and probably needed to get into a college whose entire marketing budget wasn't spent on ads in the back of TV Guide. But I never turned in my final project, probably because all it would show was exactly how much of the science I *hadn't* learned. This explains why my knowledge of physics would make an underachieving Shih Tzu look like Stephen Hawking.

Which, in turn, explains my befuddlement while watching Apollo 13 the other night. I noticed that every time the crew got in maneuvering trouble, people were terrified of "gimbal lock."

Right away that sounds bad, real bad. It sounds like something the doctor might diagnose you with after spending the previous few days bleeding from your pores:

"I'm sorry Mr. Van Winkle, it appears you have Gimbal Lock. I have to quarantine you from the entire human race ... Forever."

"Gimbal lock." That just sounds like something you NEVER want to happen—in the car, at the kitchen table, in the bathroom, on your honeymoon. Nevertheless, I wanted to know exactly what it is so I could further appreciate the heroics of our astronauts.

After Googling it and finding the simplest explanation for gimbal lock, I still lack the PhD apparently required to understand the concept. I immediately recognized words like "vector," "axis," and "degrees" as the vocabulary of my mortal enemy. Like everything in physics, "gimbal lock" is evidently a matter of national security, as there is *no* monosyllabic, non-mathematical explanation of it.

Remember: This is coming from a curious, albeit incompetent, layman. But as near as I can tell, "gimbal lock" is when all ability to maneuver is gone because each needed maneuvering force is unable to compensate for the other along an axis in reference to a fixed point.

I know ... I have no idea what I just said either. And it may very well be gibberish, anyway.

From my layman's perspective—and, *please*, do not refer your children to my understanding of this phenomenon for their science papers— "gimbal lock" means the fixed reference point needed to maneuver properly in space is lost because, in some way, there is no ability to keep the craft from an aimless, endless free-fall; you basically become a two-dimensional object in three-dimensional space.

Kind of like driving off a cliff: You can turn the wheel and stomp the brakes but because there is no friction with the ground, you have no compensatory thrust in the fall to adjust trajectory away from complete destruction.

I think.

For space craft, it evidently means that without the reference point and without the ability to maneuver the craft back in line with the fixed reference, you tumble into space, basically for eternity. This seems to explain why the boys on Apollo 13 and in Houston were so panicked about "gimbal lock."

I'm a little worried about it now, sitting in my chair.

What happens when the gimbals lock in life? I had this thought while sifting through the Googled articles.

What happens when the fixed reference by which you've navigated is lost, and you suddenly have no maneuverability to restore order? What's next when you are suddenly two-dimensional, and every attempt at correction only careens you further off into the deep molasses of silence?

I guess life is a journey and each season of life is a leg of the journey. The latest leg of my particular journey has been one of the most difficult I have ever faced.

Like the astronauts on Apollo 13, in the middle of a routine and predictable flight, I suddenly have "a problem." The causes are severe and complex and multiple and yet frustratingly imperceptible.

When one issue is finally fixed, different ones explode; when all is calm, I am most worried. The frequency and variety of these maladies has bordered on and then brazenly crossed over the border into the absurd.

And I feel at times like I am flirting with my own personal gimbal lock. I'm not completely immobile, but it seems I have a hard time maneuvering sensibly while trying to pinpoint the problem.

The other "problem" is that when I call out for Houston, there is nothing but deafening static. The reference point darts in and out of the window each morning ... I'm trying to find it again while trying to fix the problems that are wreaking havoc while calling for assistance while trying to keep the gimbals from locking completely.

I know this: I know that this situation has opened my eyes to a realm of life happily undiscovered until a few short months ago. Like a razor in your Halloween candy bar, it has sliced through innocence and is carving up idealism.

I also have a newfound admiration for those who have gone before me and landed safely; I'm sure every one of them has experienced this. Yet, my mind can't help thinking of friends who fell to such gimbal lock, both professionally and personally. I'm sick for them.

There is a loneliness and disorientation that attends such seasons in life; misery no one can adequately describe eventually slithers in as well. From here I can see exactly how good people fall off into depression, despondency, callousness, divorce ... or just quitting. On everything.

In the past, I've considered their desperation and wondered why they simply never "pulled out of it." Only now, after my crash course in physics, do I begin to understand: The problem exploded one ordinary day during a routine, predictable life, and they became so disoriented so quickly that the fundamental problem behind it all couldn't be identified before it was too late.

Nothing worked; everything froze; one solution created a variety of problems; Houston was silent; the Reference Point was gone ... Gimbal lock.

I feel bad now for thinking so ill of them then.

Will the gimbals lock in my life? I have no idea. If the movie offers any instruction, relentless determination to see tomorrow and abiding conviction that our worst day will not be *this* day keeps the fight alive.

Sound wisdom.

However, I would add faith to the list. Simply because Houston seems silent means neither that it's not there nor that it's unconcerned. Faith reminds us to trust that the Lord's hand remains over our lives, even when it can't be discerned by our senses.

That's the nature of faith; it is indeed the *"substance of things hoped for"* and *"the evidence of things not seen."* Despite sensing foreboding futility all around, faith generates hope that keeps me working the problem and pressing on while taking strength from the promise of finding joy in the end.

I may not know much physics, but I'd like to see an underachieving Shih Tzu explain that.

Faith is the Victory

Life is always easier on the drawing board. And safer. As long as the future remains there, no one gets hurt, no one fails, and no dream needs be abandoned. Much of my early adulthood was spent doodling on the drawing board, which means that I had big plans but no intentions.

One of the first times I tried to lift a plan off the drawing board and accomplish it in life, I was given an enduring lesson. Some might call it a punch in the gut; it certainly felt like every playground gut punch I absorbed as a kid.

There were actually two separate times I attempted to enroll at Baptist Bible College in Springfield, Missouri. I hated both my sojourns in the land where grammar goes to die, but the first one was mercifully shorter than the other.

I first drove down to Springfield in 1987. (Springfield is always "down," even if you're traveling from South America.) In the passenger seat was someone whose friendship I still have a hard time explaining to onlookers. An incorrigible liar and singularly focused on himself, the tidiest explanation of why we were friends is that he has always been comic relief— Porky Pig to my Daffy Duck.

Believing God would provide everything necessary that I failed to provide for myself and that colleges training pastors wouldn't let something like "filthy lucre" stand in the way of my enrollment, I arrived on campus without money on an early January Sunday evening. This was a mistake for a variety of reasons.

One, almost all Baptist churches had a Sunday evening church service in 1987, which meant we arrived to a ghost campus. We might as well have expected a noon Bacchus Feast in Tehran during Ramadan.

Even if there were no church services to attend, it was Sunday, an unlikely day to find any college administrative offices open, let alone those of a Bible college. Standing on a deserted campus, the bleak reality settled on us that we couldn't get a room.

Did I mention I had no money?

Through the pity of some students who saw us wandering like vagrants, we spent the night on the floor of a dorm room decorated in Dallas Cowboy paraphernalia. Danny White kept watch over me that evening, which is not as comforting as people from Texas might think.

I went to the offices the next morning, announcing my arrival to the good folks in charge of Baptist Bible College. They were glad to see me; they were equally glad that we were saved from the wet, stabbing air that infests southwest Missouri in January.

Oh, and they wanted their money before getting me that room.

Did I mention I had none?

Money was a part of my plan that didn't seem important on the drawing board but was explained in the Registrar's office as an urgently critical, nonnegotiable first essential. Turns out, Bible colleges need money like any other college.

I hadn't planned on this. I tried to explain to them how I was good for the money and that I was pretty sure it'd be a mistake to let something as petty as being unable to pay for tuition, and room, and board, and books, and fees keep me from God's perfect will.

They were willing to risk it.

My friend had less money than I but was determined to stay. Taking stock of my dignity and nearly empty wallet, I figured there was enough money for a couple tanks of gas and a can of Skoal. So, before even that was gone, I hopped in my '78 Subaru, grabbed a screwdriver to start the engine and headed north toward Lincoln late Monday afternoon, less than twenty-four hours after arriving in Springfield.

It was a dark trip driving back up the rabbit hole to Nebraska. The menacing, gray indifference that filled the winter evening matched my mood; I was twenty and felt like my whole life was piled behind me in heaping rubble.

Explaining to everyone who asked why I was back in Lincoln seemed to take a year, and with each telling, the thumbscrews of my failure turned a little tighter. Now living with my mom and no longer a hopeful college student preparing to turn the world upside down, finding a job was necessary.

I have had three jobs that sent me running *to* college as fast as I ran *from* high school. Each was so bereft of meaning, skill, and appreciation I could only imagine the people who remained at them for decades had been sentenced to terminal monotony in their youth for some crime against humanity.

Most of those people were decent and very nice. But I imagined them coming to terms years before with a life as emptied of meaning as their job, perhaps back when they were my age. And I could see a day coming when they clutched their chest as their heart perpetrated a mercy killing, refusing to beat one more time so its owner could be released from their prison of vanity.

One day, I saw me in them.

That day arrived once I had no choice but to take a job making pallets. Yes. Pallets.

The "no choice" part was a consequence of my arrest upon returning to Lincoln. I'd love to say that this particular arrest was for an exotic crime; espionage always sounded exotic—it sounds like an offense worthy of a conviction simply because of the name: *Espionage.*

It just has a sophisticated ring. It sounds like something people might actually envy you over. *"I regret I can't make it to the palace this evening, love; seems I've been apprehended by Interpol for Espionage."*

As it was, I was arrested for Failure to Appear after skipping town on a citation for Failure to Stop. After failing to actually enroll in college, this charge seemed cruelly appropriate, if bland. It also seemed like cosmic mockery regarding the impressive string of failures I had strung together in record time.

When I answered the unexpected knock at my mom's front door deep into a Sunday evening, for the second time in my life an officer was pointing a gun at me. I heard a dog growling to my left and a warrant was flashed in front of my face.

I learned something valuable that night about police showing up at your house with an arrest warrant. Cops don't come out in the cold, point their gun at your head, and drag their K9 companion to your stoop only to be turned away by gravely sincere promises to show up next time or groveling assurances that you'll take care of it in the morning.

That dog is hoping for a chance to eat your arm, and they're taking you to jail. Period.

The officer was kind enough to let me tell my mom what was going on. For the second time in her life, I was waking her from sleep to inform her there were police in the living room; moms don't appreciate this.

Spread-eagled over the hood of the patrol car, I was frisked and handcuffed. The officer and I had a nice chat on the way downtown after he made certain the cuffs weren't too tight. He recognized I wasn't a hardened criminal but always handled me a little like Charles Manson, just in case.

Mug shots and finger prints in the system, I used my one call to wake the only person I knew at the time who had the means to post bail. He groggily agreed to put up the money, and I was left to wait in an area that resembled a seedy hotel waiting room with the evening's other prisoners.

The seats were hard, white plastic and the carpet was spotted with crunchy stains and we had a nice view of the cells where the truly hardened criminals were stored. The only other thing in the room was a pay phone attached to a concrete column thick enough to stop a bullet train and seemingly anchored down into the earth's crust.

A woman was on the phone, yelling at whoever was on the other end about needing cocaine. If the tone of her voice and apparent disregard about screaming a request for illicit drugs into a jailhouse phone was any indication, I'd say she needed some cocaine pretty badly.

Waiting for my bail, I wondered how I got there. How did I go from a dream life in the mountains of Montana among new friends, to pursuing a call to enter ministry, to sitting on a plastic bench listening to a madwoman demand coke in the Lincoln City Jail … to being horrified at what I just put my hand in that was oozing from under the bench.

No answer came, but my bail did.

On the way home, my bondsman told me he could get me a job making pallets. Since pawning a shotgun the next morning was my only way of paying fines and being unsure of what kind of job I could get as an "ex-con," it seemed I had no choice.

Pallets are like lots of things everyone takes for granted. Toothpaste caps, clothes hangers, and paper towel tubes are all similar to pallets in that we never conceive that a human being would actually spend their life making them. They just appear, as from fairies, we assume, because no one grows up hoping to make clothes hangers or paper towel tubes their life's work.

I'm living proof, however, that actual people spend at least some of their lives producing such things. ˙

With my tail between my legs, I showed up every morning to a dingy shanty-factory west of Lincoln, cloistered behind cottonwoods and out of sight of polite company. I'm pretty sure it would have made OSHA's Most Wanted List and had the look of ground zero for some kind of illegal activity.

But there wasn't. It was just pallets.

In bitter cold that slowed molecules enough to actually see them trying to maintain cohesion, I stood and cut logs on a saw the diameter of a hula-hoop that had all safety measures removed. The man we worked for had several fingers missing.

We rolled cottonwood trunks massive enough to house several elfin families onto a conveyor belt with crowbars, hoping none would overshoot and crush one of us charged with keeping it from rolling off the belt. I stopped an errant trunk one afternoon with my finger; I yanked it out from beneath the trunk so fast, I think the log itself was surprised. Lifting it to my eyes, my prayers must have been answered mid-air because there was not so much as a bruise on a finger that should have been severed instantly.

I would have quit then, but I had nothing else to do. My bones froze every morning; I distracted myself with nail-gun fights in the afternoon (don't try this at home, or anywhere else) and felt sorry for myself all night.

And for the first time in years, I hadn't been to church for several months. This was the capstone of the worst personal disorientation I've ever experienced. Weak, cynical, dazed, and only twenty-one years old, I felt exiled from hope and a stranger in my own life.

No matter how reasonable it seems at the time, I've never known *not* going to church to solve anything. I've never seen abandoning faith or fleeing from people who care make life more tolerable. But anger with God masquerading as self-pity is more enjoyable than anyone wants to admit and twice as hard to quit.

It felt as though I had abandoned everything that made me me, especially my faith. There's something necessary about faith in life. Without it, all we have is what we have, and that's a disheartening prospect when life yields nothing but bleakness.

What I've noticed over time is that turning points are often disguised as points of no return, especially when people are stringing together an impressive streak of failures: One too many failures, and we lose all ability to find victory.

Failure is about life; faith is about victory. The turning point of my failures in 1987 wasn't about determination or about luck. It was about reclaiming the one thing that makes life wonderful because it transforms life into a prelude, not a finale: Faith.

It will sound simplistic, but I recaptured my faith in community with believers, and things turned around. I got a new job; I found and married the love of my life; I made it to and through college.

There's an old hymn that comforts, *"faith is the victory that overcomes the world."* Failure seems like an endless road at times; just when it appeared mine stretched far over the horizon, I found a turning point.

Not because I pulled myself up, but because, from the pit of my own failures, I finally looked up to find hope held out.

He Did Faithful Well

This is an eventful year. Not only is it twenty years since I graduated from college, it's the twentieth year since a young couple named Steve and Cheryl moved to Bozeman so Steve could be Youth Pastor for $75.00/week at Fellowship Baptist Church.

That wasn't the first ministry job I accepted in 1992, however. Before Bozeman, there was Lincoln; before Fellowship, there was Plains.

Pastor Dan Inman of Plains Baptist Church in Lincoln was my first boss out of college; I received his offer twenty years ago this week. Our agreement was simple: Come work for him for zero dollars a week, and I would never again have to live in a place where "*'ns*" is considered an appropriate contraction for 1st, 2nd, and 3rd person personal pronouns.

We'ns immediately left southwest Missouri.

Pastor Inman had taken over the church my friend Dirt and I discovered several years earlier after we were sent fleeing Springfield like the hapless sons of Sceva in the book of Acts. For me, Plains Baptist is a warehouse of memories that reads like an ecclesiastical "St. Elsewhere."

These unforgettable episodes include a Sunday our pastor was taking prayer requests. One of our regulars delivered newspapers early Sunday mornings and raised her hand in response to his invitation: *"Please pray for the man who flashed me this morning."*

What do you say to that? How do you pray for it?

In these worship services, the sound of belches were as routine as "amens" during the morning sermon. The elder statesman of our congregation wore an American flag print tie matched to a gray-pinstriped, white polyester suit—*every* Sunday. I watched a person make change in the offering plate being passing—seriously, make change.

The walls were infested with bees. The balcony hosted only ghosts from the past, and we all gathered dutifully every Sunday and Wednesday in the rickety remnant of a once-proud turn-of-the-century American Methodist Episcopal brick building that had become a refuge for a variety of theological refugees through the decades.

Still, it was our church. I brought Cheryl to it when we first started dating; it's where she was baptized after meeting Christ and where we were married. While attending between my first and second year of college, the pastor we loved and who married us suddenly resigned soon after our wedding in the summer of 1990.

By then, the church had fallen into disrepair in every way imaginable— physically, spiritually, financially. The Gothic building on 29th and Randolph in my hometown was, frankly, a shell of what it was and even what it should have been.

Before departing, our pastor told us there was a minister in Vermont interested in the position. I was twenty-four and one of only three or four men on the "pulpit committee" tasked with finding a new pastor for our church.

We had a more pressing question to consider first: Should we disband or continue?

The church was down to twenty-five people or so, and Cheryl and I were leaving soon and going back to college. Because of this, I recused myself from voting on the matter; however, I did express my thoughts about whether Plains could continue as a going concern. I also questioned the wisdom of asking a man and his wife to move two-thousand miles and take a church that didn't notice its own toe-tag dangling off the gurney.

"How can we pay for his move?" I asked.

"But this church has been such a blessing to so many people," replied the roly-poly man who hadn't worked a job since I knew him.

"Really? Where are they? Will they pay his moving expense? His salary? Our current pastor hasn't been paid since … well, ever."

"But this church can't fold; it has to keep going. We CAN'T let it die."

Speaking of personal pronouns, sometimes the loudest people use the first person plural ("we") when they really mean the second person plural ("you"). This man's exclamation, therefore, would be more accurately phrased, *"You can't let it die."*

Knowing this, I pressed, *"Okay; I'll go along with it if you will pledge to attend all services and get a job to help provide the financial support needed to give a new pastor and this church a chance."*

"Well ... maybe we better not." Bingo.

I don't remember the rest of the details of that conversation, but I think the other guys suggested we have this interested lunatic come and check out our church. The idea being that only *God* could convince someone to trade a congregation in Vermont for this sinkhole in Nebraska.

That pastor was Dan Inman. When I saw him, my first thought was, *"Holy cow, that guy is huge."* He dwarfed most everyone in every direction the human body could grow.

Sunday, he preached to a crowd of 30. The pulpit committee joined him and his wife, Jeannie, for lunch afterward at the home of a lovable older lady named Virginia whose cherry blintzes would make Satan speak in tongues. Over dessert, we learned the Inmans were from Kansas and they wanted to be closer to home; the proximity of Lincoln to their home state was a big reason for their interest.

Maybe it was Virginia's blintzes, but before leaving her house, he said he was ready to be the next pastor if we would have him. Since the only qualifications we established were that a candidate fog a mirror and be willing to come, the pulpit committee met once more.

Still not voting and still clinging to my Catch-22 perspective that anyone who *wanted* this church was unfit for *any* church, I reiterated my concerns about the people's commitment. However, the folks at Plains Baptist figured anyone who wanted them must be God's man.

Thus began Dan Inman's final assignment: Salvaging the wreck of the SS Plains.

When Cheryl and I finally made it to Lincoln after taking the position at Plains, we set about sprucing up the very dated and dilapidated structure, hoping that the limping outpost would seem more welcoming to the few normal people who occasionally visited. Most everyone who had "committed" to support the new pastor two years earlier was gone by the time we arrived—big surprise.

Yet, with an indefatigable smile I never fully understood, Pastor Inman managed to eke a little hope out of the remnant clinging to the tragic belief Plains wouldn't die. He did so neither with inspiring oratory nor dynamic personality, but by simply continuing to do all the mundane things that keep churches going.

In the midst of this steadfastness, he suffered his first cardiac event. Like I said, he was large but not in the body-builder kind of way.

He determined to get healthier after being released from the hospital. For years, a mountain bike was my primary transportation after I hastily abandoned my '78 Subaru in a grocery store parking lot (but that's another story). Pursuing his second chance at health, Pastor Inman decided a bike would do him good as well; he purchased one and suggested we go riding around town together.

The first time we did was memorable. I was greeted at the parsonage by one of the funniest sights I have ever seen.

Pastor Inman's new bike had evidently been modified by a kid named Poindexter who enjoyed spending his free time reading up on public safety. His advanced all-terrain bike sported a little horn to alert other riders, mirrors on the handlebars and a tall, orange flag; the only thing missing was playing cards in the spokes.

Astride it was this rather large man with a helmet that looked a size-and-a-half too small that sported yet another side-view mirror. He wore gloves and, in my memory, I think he was wearing riding shorts—spandex riding shorts.

I confess to having more than a few laughs over this through the years. I mention it now because as I have gotten older, not only do I pray I never look like that, but because I recognize the sort of courage it took for an upper middle-aged man to try something as foreign as biking, probably knowing he would stick out a little. Or a lot.

It's the same kind of courage that I imagine led him to take a surefire disaster of a church and see value where I found disgust and to look for life where I was certain only death resided. Dan Inman did something at Plains Baptist Church I'm not sure anyone else could have: He waited out its death looking for a resurrection.

He did it with what, in hindsight, I see as steady-handedness and godly patience, and he received his rightful reward of witnessing that resurrection. I don't know much about present-day Plains Baptist Church, but I do know that Pastor Inman left it a *much* better place than he found it.

I wish all of us could say the same about our jobs, homes, and friends.

Pastor Inman died this week.

Twenty years after I left for Montana and twenty-two years after arriving in Lincoln, he died, having, in fact, salvaged Plains Baptist Church. Along the way, Dan Inman's life taught me something about trust. He showed me that it is the fruit of honor, that there is no shortcut to establish it, that there is nothing left when it is violated.

I've told each of my kids that nothing is so valuable and fragile between us as trust. I've told couples, both married and soon-to-be-married, that relationships run on trust, not love; love is nice, but violate trust and you have nothing left.

Pastor Inman was a man you could trust in every way and with everything imaginable. You could trust him to tell the truth, to work when no one else cared, to do the hard things no one wanted to do. He held precious things in an inviolable trust, like his family and his congregation.

Trust is the legacy of faithfulness.

Dan Inman was never recognized as wildly successful in his vocation; he never interviewed Presidents; he never wrote a book nor gave counsel to power brokers. But what he did, he did faithfully. He was faithful to his wife and family, to his church and his friends, and to his Lord.

The bulk of America is made up of Dan Inmans. They are the equivalent of what George Bailey reminded Mr. Potter were the vast majority of people who do *"most of the working and paying and living and dying in this community."*

People like Pastor Inman aren't limited to churches or pastorates. They aren't noticed often nor celebrated much, but they do most of the loving and caring and working and sacrificing around us, and only the people who have come into close contact with them are able to take up the task of remembering their faithfulness in life.

I remember. I remember Pastor Inman doing his ministering and caring and serving and forgiving ... faithfully.

Pastor Dan Inman did faithful very well.

The Baseline of Life

I've been watching the news more lately. You probably have too. If we compare notes, we'd probably have the same impressions. There's less work, more uncertainty, and a general feeling of foreboding about 2009. Watching all the hand-wringing over the economy, it seems this New Year is beginning with something that no other has in recent memory: two strikes.

I have heard and seen a lot of people take some stock of what's happening. Many people have learned lessons, and many more are searching for some. It's not always easy to maintain perspective when the economy seems to be collapsing, especially considering that for nearly fifteen years or so, the culture has blared at us that the bottom-line is the standard by which we should be reviewing our lives.

I think, however, that I have reason to consider a baseline of life most of those experiencing inconsolable grief over the economy never factor. The thought occurred to me in an unusual place.

My wife, Cheryl, and I were with a church member whose family owns one of the oldest ranches in Montana. He invited us up to hunt elk over Thanksgiving weekend; my usual luck prevailed as we only saw a great big herd of Jack Squat.

We were roaming up on a high plateau overlooking the entire valley, which brought us eye-level with some of the purple mountains' majesty hundreds of miles away. Bouncing over ruts only Pinocchio could label as roads, we traveled an old stagecoach trail through a high meadow. We drifted through old homesteads littering the choicest ground now dusted with snow under an obscenely blue sky while the wind was knocking the sage over and pushing around ancient pines.

And, something captured my thoughts up there.

I could see peaks above me. They were close by, and the valley was "out there," far below my elevated view; I was high up, and yet I was in a kind of a bowl.

I thought that, if I hadn't known better, if I hadn't kept track of how far up I had traveled, I would look up from this plateau and think it was a valley. I was looking around at the grandeur and realized how my perspective on life had been altered.

I have whined and complained this past year; I have felt the depth of despair and despondency; I have learned to distrust myself and re-learned lessons good men had taught me years before. But, the journey to and the view from that high plateau on the Climbing Arrow Ranch helped me. It helped me regain perspective.

I reminded myself that the valleys I trudge through are indeed long and far below the peak … but maybe … the valleys are actually high plateaus far above all the sorrow and misery and pain and lostness and loneliness and addiction and depression that could have defined my life had God not lifted me high above the actual valley's floor.

And here I was, in a place where only a privileged few get to go without paying thousands of dollars, and I lived in a place that only a privileged few get to call home. I pastor a church of people I am privileged to know, and I have a family that I have a hard time writing about simply because I do not possess the vocabulary to describe my love and my satisfaction and my awe and my gratitude for them; my wife still sleeps beside me.

I have made friends of indescribably interesting people and discovered brothers-in-arms in the ministry and have met men along the way I cherish more than they'll ever know. I can look out my window and watch a sky bleed to the ground over the peaks of the Bridger Mountains, and I can stop on my way home and catch brown trout in high-def colors while mottled fall leaves drop like rain around me in an autumn breeze.

The world may crash around me, but I can hear my daughter sing and feel the wetness of a tear, and I can make less money than I did a year ago but know I've received a raise in blessings. I can see that God has the final say in everything even if I think I know the reason or the future.

I can watch Nebraska football with my son and smile as I pass on a sweet addiction to him. And I can read the scripture and wonder at how it speaks to me still, and I can stand to preach at one of the worst times in our Nation's economic history and sense that I have something to say from God.

I have navigated fifteen years of ministry in one church without having to sell used cars, and I have known the Lord for twenty-five years and I've never gone to bed hungry. I can read the sticky notes my daughter leaves on my desk telling me how much she loves me.

And suddenly, I see my life for *where* it is: far, far above the tragedies in the valley below.

Perhaps I forget from time to time that slugging through a plateau just beneath the peak is infinitely better than being condemned to the valley. I think I too often take for granted how high up God has taken my life and how far up He has planted my feet; consequently, I am prone to look at the plateaus like they were the valley.

It doesn't mean the plateaus aren't hard or painful—they are. I have never experienced such madness and uncertainty and anger and apathy as I have this past year. It's just that, every now and then, I need to remind myself that, because of Christ, I will never see the actual valley floor again.

While the world at large measures its own worth by the bottom line, *this* is the baseline of the Christian life.

It doesn't mean the economy won't crash or trials can be avoided or people won't lose their jobs. It means that, for believers, these things happen far above the valley floor, where heaven is a real promise and brothers and sisters in Christ are genuine comfort and hope buoys all because Jesus loved us and died for us.

No one knows what a day may bring forth, let alone a year. But while the bottom line may be fickle as economies adjust and times change, the baseline of our life in Christ stabilizes our perspective and keeps our hope constant, no matter what circumstances 2009 will bring upon us all.

CHAPTER 5

··

PROVIDENCE & COMPASSION

It's All Right

I wonder if you have the same memories I do: The sweet, electric whiff of pine mingled with hot, painted bulbs in a dark room bathed in their glow and light-hearted yet warm decorations hung in defiance of the stark reality normally residing there. Most of all, I remember an anticipation for things only possible this time of year.

In thirty-nine years, I now have a pocketful of Christmases from which to draw memories; some of them shine brighter than others. Like most people's, a number of these holidays passed with hasty obscurity, almost as if we awoke one morning to find a tree growing out of our carpet with boxes strewn on the floor.

If you asked me which mornings represent the high-water marks of my childhood Christmases, two come to mind instantly. The first, when I was about seven, began in the usual manner with my bolting awake in the pre-dawn darkness. Instead of having to endure the usual torment of waiting for my parents to crawl out of bed, however, the living room lights were already on. And my grandpa was there, which was unusual.

He lived thirty miles from us; thirty miles in 1973 seemed more like three hundred today. He was a depot agent on the railroad, assuring I would cultivate a lifelong love of trains; to this day, I still look at them with the eyes of a kid.

On this Christmas morning I found a somewhat empty tree awaiting me, but I hadn't been to the basement, which, I suppose, isn't surprising. Christmas morning is about presents and childhood greed, neither of which had anything to do with our "hoongy" basement, as my mom would say.

Nevertheless, I was escorted down there by my grandpa.

As we descended the steps, two 4 x 8 sheets of plywood lined with track and one American Flyer train ready to glide out of the station greeted me. I played all day, dropping off passengers, hauling freight, and seeing the world from the cab of my American Flyer locomotive.

I don't know why I remember this next one. Maybe I wanted the present so badly that the thrill of finally getting it never goes away. I'm sure I circled it heavily in our Sears Christmas Wishbook, and under the tree that Christmas morning was the object of my holiday desire: NFL Electric Football—a vibrating, metal football field with plastic men and felt footballs.

I never mastered it; mostly, my players ran in circles. My friend Jerry Myers beat me at it mercilessly. I think one of Jerry's plastic tailbacks is still running for a touchdown somewhere in Nova Scotia by now.

But what a morning it was when I finally laid that metal field out in front of me.

Along with everything else, Christmas changed after my dad left us; indeed, the makeup of life changed. Money was scarce and emotions were frayed. It seemed a perpetual, low-grade earthquake had shaken the context of our days loose from the moorings of security.

Except for Christmas.

Christmas was a break from the coldness and sparseness that defined our reality. This should not be confused with actually having the necessities we lived without the previous fifty-one weeks of the year. It just seemed that, at Christmas, there was an inescapable feeling that everything was going to be all right.

Most childhood Christmas memories are about gifts or grandparents, as my previous recollections attest. Yet, for me, there is a particular Christmas from these unsettled times that remains vivid in my memory, and it has nothing to do with anything wrapped in festive paper.

The Christmas trees at friends' houses were always loaded with presents. Their families were together, and everyone was preparing for a holiday surrounded by loved ones and marked by abundance. I don't know if their Christmases were actually anything like this, but it certainly appeared that way.

The apparent abundance in my friends' homes made me feel a little poorer than I actually was, mainly because I always went home to a house that lacked much of the material trappings of the holiday. When you're twelve or thirteen, there is little comfort in the "meaning" of the season; the trappings *are* the meaning.

One thing we were able to do, however, was find a little solace from that Christmas notion of everything being all right. This license to claim a reprieve from the fatigue of reality—even if only for a week or two—was present enough for a family living in want. It was the sweetest gift of all.

I hardly ever speak about my hard luck as a kid. There are stories of genuine poverty many, many times more desperate than mine that, by comparison, make my childhood look ridiculously privileged. Still, it is not an embellishment to characterize our house as often being thin on food and short on money for essentials.

We weren't starving; let's just say that before the end of each month, you could hear echoes inside our cupboards. So, after paying December's necessities, little money was left over for more than a smattering of Christmas presents.

Actually, there probably was no money for gifts, but some always showed up anyway.

This is the reason we had resigned ourselves to wait on getting a tree until maybe Christmas Eve when weary vendors looked to offload their remnant of pines like zucchini in the summer. I don't know how, but our neighbors took note of our treeless living room and came over on a Saturday morning two weeks before Christmas.

They said they were going out to buy their tree and wanted us to come along so they could get ours as well. More than 25 years later, I still see their gift standing in our bland but heavily decorated living room, casting a warmth across the house I cannot fully describe even today.

My tennis shoes were so ratty that winter, they looked like I put them in a Waring blender every morning before slipping into them. I'm sure my sister's weren't far behind; we wore things until there was no way to tie, strap, zip, or button them on.

Someone from the church we attended noticed our socks sticking out the gaps and told my mom they wanted to buy my sister and me new shoes. We went to Sears and picked pairs that I'm sure were too expensive and probably made us both look ungrateful; nevertheless, we wore them home. I don't remember the woman who took us, but Ruby Slippers were never more appreciated than the sneakers I wore home from Sears.

Then, Christmas Eve, a knock on our door was opened to my mom's boss standing on our stoop. He was an insurance executive and held out a giant wad of tinfoil. She stood there for a time and, after several minutes of talk and gestures, came in with tears in her eyes, clutching the wad of foil. Christmas dinner had just been given to us, she said; a turkey was inside the silver ball of Reynolds wrap.

Later into the night, as we were getting ready to go to church, I saw a friend run up into our yard. It was dark outside, and the headlights from his parents' Ford Galaxy shone behind him as he ran up to our front door through the glow of the colored lights hung along our roofline. Draped in a thick coat, he reached the concrete stoop and knocked.

I opened the door with my mom and sister nearby, and John stepped in with two giant, overflowing bags of groceries. My mom pored through the contents with an amalgamated look of glee and relief washing over her face. If her reaction to two bags of groceries was any indication, we probably would have eaten our gifted turkey the next day with nothing but water.

I loved my trains, and memories of Electric Football usher me back to a carefree childhood. But I never had a better Christmas than the one when we decorated a tree bought by neighbors, wore shoes given by people who cared, cooked a turkey provided by someone who had plenty, and received two bags of groceries delivered by a twelve-year-old who had taken note of a bare kitchen and decided he could do something about it.

These are the gifts that forever sealed the certainty in my heart that, at Christmas, everything was going to be all right.

But it also impressed on me the value of a cup of cold water to those who thirst. Remembering the people who inserted themselves between us and despair thirty-some years ago is a humbling yet complete joy. Truly, some of the best gifts I ever received at Christmas were generated from deep wells of compassion found in the heart of ordinary people.

I can't help but think as well that the people who supplied them would probably say those were the best gifts they ever gave. My guess is that they never felt better about themselves than when they helped a family who had need thrust into their lives. They might say they never knew a brighter, more satisfying Christmas than when their care and generosity comforted a young, struggling family by assuring them, *"It's all right, we're here."*

And that's in keeping with the grand message of Christmas itself, isn't it? Christmas is God the Father looking down on an obscure night upon a pedestrian settlement in Palestine watching His Son take on flesh so He could walk among, touch, and bestow hope on the spiritually bankrupt.

This spirit of the original Christmas passes down the unshakable belief in what should be while also compelling acts of heroic generosity from ordinary people. In the cry that echoed out of a manger, a lost creation found hope that defied its condition and comfort that can satisfy a soul.

In that first Christmas, God says to the world what the generosity and kindness of others said to my family during Christmas, 1978. It has always been true: Christmas is God's assurance to the impoverished and spiritually needy.

"It's all right. I'm here."

A Lifetime in Her Song

I read somewhere some time ago that the number one fear people have is public speaking; I think fear of flying was, like, number three. Depending on what statistic list you consult, some fear public speaking with the same intensity of terror as death itself.

I hate flying; chemistry has made even the thought of getting on a plane tolerable for me. Because something so common generally terrifies me, people love to mock my perfectly reasonable aversion to being drilled into the earth from 30,000 feet inside a winged coffin.

They aren't so chatty, however, when I hand over a microphone and invite them to give the week's sermon. So, I retort, since my job involves engaging the number *one* fear three times a *week*, I'm entitled to a pass for my anxiety over number *three* every *now and then*.

In my vocation, preaching is the centerpiece; preachers gonna preach, as it were. What's easily missed about this is that neither tragedies nor elations qualify as excused absences from coming to "work"; indeed, these things call all the more for my presence.

I've preached funerals, and, even more frightening, I've officiated at weddings. I've preached after Presidential scandals inflamed the nation, and I've preached to wounded congregations in the wake of a pastor's ugly resignation. I've preached with heaviness on my heart for others and pity in my heart for me.

Like so many others who oversee churches across the globe, I have come to a pulpit on Sunday morning and opened a Bible to preach, all the while knowing I stood between a congregation and the countless varieties of life's pain and personal trauma. And there have been mornings that pain and trauma lurked within me.

These are the Sundays I faithfully put on a game face before the assembly so I could be "God's man" for the morning. Every Sunday morning for years, whether filled with joy or nursing my own wounds, I guess you could say that I did my job.

Until this Sunday.

I walked to the platform after a stirring rendition of the final hymn our congregation sung together, "It is Well with My Soul." The last verse was a cappella, and it evoked a flood of indescribable emotions I knew were going to be a problem for me.

People were seated, and I asked them to turn to the text for the sermon. As they did, I started to say how thankful I was for the special solo we enjoyed before "It is Well."

I started to ...

Suddenly, I couldn't look at the people; it was as though my forehead were attached to a cord on the pulpit and someone was pulling it downward. I felt the wet warmth of tears pooling in and leaking from my eyelids. My lungs starting to take short, quick movements as if in a sprint to catch the emotions spilling out of my eyes.

Speaking was impossible; I felt my throat quickly constrict each time I tried to eke out a word. I opened my mouth, desperately hoping to continue, but all I could do was suck in air. I played with the ribbon in my Bible, trying to look like I had something to do besides weep uncontrollably.

Standing there, for the first time ever, I seriously thought I wasn't going to be able to compose myself. Each attempt at forming a word ended with my emotions snatching the last few consonants down my throat. All I could do was try to keep from completely breaking down.

The people patiently waited for me to come back to the business at hand, but that wasn't likely in the immediate future. Minutes passed, each seeming like hours. I was staring at the pages of my Bible, but, in my mind, I was re-living my entire life.

I thought about my childhood in Lincoln, Nebraska, a childhood interrupted and an adulthood hastened by the departure of my dad. I thought of how my life seemed to begin the day he ended his marriage to my mom. I remembered my mom struggling to pay bills and struggling even harder to keep herself composed at the prospect of raising two kids by herself on a secretary's skinny salary. I thought about how so many people in the position I was in at age twelve don't turn out as fortunately as I have.

In the way God created only the human mind with the ability to do, I witnessed all my life in a flashing moment. I thought again about all the roads that sprawled out before me and how each of them held so much promise so long ago. I thought about how so many of my friends who took different, seemingly opportunistic paths now have shattered lives, broken families, and daily heartache. Some are even dead, believing the lie that whatever life laid beyond this one, there is no way it could be worse.

I thought about meeting my wife, about the days when she was only my girlfriend. I recalled all she has put up with in the name of love and how I have so feebly and so seldom repaid her in kind. I thought of her dad dying last summer and how, even now, she still grieves with a sincerity that has helped me understand the true sense of the word "loss."

I tried to wipe away the tears, but it felt like the liquid saturation of using a soaked paper towel to wipe up a new spill on the counter. Running fingers across my eyelids only pushed tears away to be instantly replaced by new ones.

I think I apologized to everyone; I was taking their time to have a personal breakdown. I recall hearing a few "amens" and "that's alrights." They are a gracious collection of people, but their graciousness only gave me license to indulge even more memories standing in line for their turn at the well of tears.

I thought about how God unexpectedly took a nondescript kid in a pedestrian city and saved me when all the odds were against me. He pulled me from the ranks not only of the spiritually lost but the culturally lost, for no other reason than because that is Who He is: The rescuer of misfits and Savior of sinners.

I thought about how much I haven't thought about this in recent memory.

I thought about a new Christian, 19 years old, driving to Montana with $50.00 in his pocket in January of 1985. This 19-year-old never had much use for church; I thought about how that young man happened to meet a pastor who was starting a new church in Bozeman. I remembered my baptism 16 years ago in that church which I now pastor.

I recalled thinking how amazing it would be if God would use me in His church. And what if He would call me into the ministry. I remembered the privilege I sensed in the infancy of my ministry to deliver His word, marveling daily at God's using me in any way.

I thought, again, about how much time had passed since I thought of such a thing.

Standing there for a few awkward minutes, restraining tears before the Sunday morning congregation, I was overcome with thankfulness. And I eventually pressed on with the morning's message; however, I don't think I stopped wiping the tears out of my eyes until the second point of my sermon.

But the story would be incomplete without revealing why I was so overcome with irresistible emotions: It was the solo before our last hymn.

It wasn't grand in scale nor was it handsomely performed by an orchestra or majestic organ. It wasn't even a complicated tune. It was the singer.

She sang a two-verse rendition of "Oh How He Loves You and Me," and when I heard it, I was lost in thankfulness for my life, God's grace, and all the blessings so callously neglected every day. This singer brought my heart to its knees as God used her to show me once again His glory and goodness and mercy to me.

The soloist was my eight-year-old daughter, Madison, standing alone before a microphone singing of the love of God that touched her dad eighteen years ago. I lived my life over again in her song and was overwhelmed that she was where she was today because God was where I was eighteen years before.

Gratitude so filled my heart for God's work of grace in my life that had saved me, saved my wife, and now was touching my kids that the only words I could choke out of my tear-stained voice were,

"I'm so thankful that I met Christ eighteen years ago. I'm so thankful I walked into this church sixteen years ago. The greatest blessing I have known as a parent is to hear my daughter sing to the Lord, and I hope all of you get a chance to know it as well someday."

I think those words after my involuntary display of thankfulness accomplished more than the thirty-minute sermon I stumbled through the rest of the morning.

My eight-year-old daughter taught me a profound lesson in the words of one of the simplest songs ever composed. Living a lifetime over again in her song, I was confronted with a lesson on God's amazing, yet subtle, grace over time; namely, that it is easily forgotten once people become familiar with miracles and comfortable with their conversion.

Only God could have salvaged my life; only my daughter could have been used by Him to soften and swell my heart with thankfulness once again.

Madison, oh how He loves you and me.

I wrote this down, so I could share it with her one day.

The Last Compassion

Ten years ago this month, I went on my only overseas mission trip with a group of people from our church. We went to South Africa.

For me, the best thing we did while there was put on a carnival for kids in an AIDS orphanage. There were two kinds of children there: those who had been orphaned because their parents died of AIDS and those who had been orphaned because they had been born with AIDS.

As I was thinking of the next story for a blog I created, I remembered something that happened that afternoon a decade ago, after we were all exhausted by fun and steeped in guilty satisfaction over bringing a little happiness to such a pain-saturated place.

Little South Africans were running around laughing and playing and making much ado about what we consider nothing. In addition to the games and toys, however, perhaps their absolute favorite thing to do was sit on our laps.

Below are a couple of journal entries from that day and from that experience:

"*Uneasiness ... Several kids obviously wanted nothing more than to sit on my lap, really—the people who care for them seem attentive and affectionate, but I guess little kids never get enough of sitting on laps ... The uneasiness was from the fact that I sensed this is what they really wanted and what I simply could not give them ... more than candy or toys or carnivals, it felt as though these kids sat on my lap the way people sit on seats in a plane: expecting to be winged away to a better place ... My lap was occupied for a good hour.*

After ten years, I read this and remember a very tenderhearted staff caring for these children; these kids had all the comforts of home. Except for parents. I have to wonder if desiring to be "winged off" was less about them than it was about me.

Grappling with how little we could accomplish for these children, how doing so little made us feel so much better about ourselves, I wanted to remove them from a future scarred by a modern pestilence. Maybe all they wanted was an arm wrapped around them, but I wanted to rescue them.

"It's strange how God works ... In a rare moment when I was sitting empty-lapped in the sandbox, I saw a child wandering around the sand apart from the others ... thin hair, discolored skin, smears of snot under the nose and blisters on the cheeks ... it was apparent the child had AIDS. I remember thinking how sad and even unappealing this kid looked compared to the others ... then, of course, he came over to me. He looked me in the eye, turned around, and backed on to my lap. He then grabbed my arm and flung it around his chest ... and never left. I was overwhelmed."

I remembered this because such warmth in 2004 was made possible by the African-American man sporting a bow tie peering in my office window in 1995.

I think everyone in any vocation that comes into close orbit of any kind of human triage lives on the edge. Not the edge of excitement nor danger, they live on the edge of being hopelessly drained of all caring— what I call "The Last Compassion."

It's when a person, after being lied to one too many times, allows themselves to believe all tragedy is manufactured. It's when the eager altruists sense they're being taken and have been from the beginning. It's when one of the faithful holds outstretched arms to someone hurting only to have that person sink a shiv in their back.

The Last Compassion is the caring equivalent to Apollo 13's dreaded gimbal lock. Once it happens, there's no going back; there's no chance to restore sensitivity to a heart nor vulnerability to a spirit. We become two-dimensional people in a three-dimensional calling.

I can't say how many times I feared I had expended the Last Compassion. There's a part of me that thinks it happened long ago and that all my compulsions to care are nothing more than job requirements, like an accountant can crunch numbers and never actually care about the people they represent.

While most anyone can experience it, pastors slain by this malady go through all the motions of caring and even act to supply people's needs, but they don't *actually* care. It's just their job.

I don't doubt such a confession will be used against me one day.

At my desk typing on this sparkling summer late morning over a decade ago, I had done battle with Nazis and liars and predators of kindness. I was jaded before I was thirty. I didn't know what to call it then, but it felt every bit like the hardening associated with the Last Compassion.

I often have headphones on when I'm typing; it helps me find a rhythm of thought. When I did this at the church, I'd lock the other doors of the building if I wasn't expecting anyone, because headphones are also the leading cause of fright-induced cardiac arrests when people decide to just drop by.

Since the people most likely to "drop by" were the duplicitous looking for money, I felt justified in locking the doors to God's house. But the window was still open.

His interruption distracted me from my sermonizing, which annoyed me. Turning to the sound, the best way to describe the scene was, unusual.

It was unusual to have someone tapping on my window. He was unusually short, and it was unusual to see an African-American in Bozeman.

To give some perspective about demographics here, I once had a church member invite me to lunch so we could talk about something he found troubling. A recent transplant from Georgia, he moved here to become principal of a local elementary school. By the time we met, however, he had already decided to return to Atlanta, largely because he didn't want his young children growing up in a place with so little racial diversity.

It's a fair observation. Census stats tell us, of the thirty-nine thousand people living here, only *one-half of one percent* is African American; the only racial population in Bozeman with a lower percentage is Pacific Islanders. I'm sure things have improved since the mid-nineties, but it's certainly not Atlanta in terms of cultural diversity. Or even Fargo.

Which is why I mention this man's skin color: It's unimportant except for the fact it was so unusual for Bozeman.

I could see a black bow tie on his white shirt just above the bottom ledge of my office window. He was smiling and waving. He beckoned toward the door, which I unlocked and opened. Like everyone, he held out his hand in greeting and introduced himself. I don't remember his name.

One of the symptoms of the Last Compassion is enduring every single chatty word with strangers like each one is a root canal in itself. You just want to get to the real reason people are being so friendly so you can say no and go on about your day.

"Are you the pastor?"
"Yes."

In a strictly personal protest, I had begun refusing to give my name unless someone asked for it. It was my way of denying cheats access to my humanity.

One thing gaining this man a hearing others wouldn't have was that he was dressed in black-tie formal, which is not attire you often see at 10 or 11 a.m. on a weekday; in fact, I've never seen it since. He was about five feet tall and looked like he was ready to take First Chair in the Symphony.

Like I said, it was unusual.

"I know you must hear this a lot…" (I also hear "I know you must hear this a lot" a lot) *"but I could use a little help."*

"I'm sorry, but we don't have any money." I was getting ready to send him to … well, you know where.

"I don't need much. Just $18."

He had a round, friendly, almost sympathetic face. I knew I shouldn't be taken in by it, but he seemed genuine—not his need, but his embarrassment. If there is one thing I learned in all the requests for help it is that those who really need it are not comfortable asking for it.

"$18?"

"Yes. Only enough to get a bus ticket to Butte."

At the risk of seeming insensitive, this had now gone from unusual to bizarre. Short, black men in bow ties are not often heading toward Butte, let alone intending to get off there.

"To Butte? You're going to Butte?"

"Yes. I know you must hear this a lot."

No. Actually, I didn't.

It still didn't change the fact I had no money. I had no wallet, no checkbook, and church checks required two signatures.

I had one test to see if what he asked for was legit, *"If I have it, I'll only buy a ticket. I won't give you cash."*

Usually, people don't straight up ask for cash; they ask for things and hope to get the cash to purchase them. They then go and buy all the vices humanity has invented to ruin lives with money intended to salvage them.

When you tell such people you won't give cash but will only go with them and buy their groceries, send money directly to the power company, or go to the gas station and purchase fuel, 99% stall and say they don't want to inconvenience you. When you insist, they usually get angry because you don't believe them and stomp out protesting the way you have insulted their dignity.

"That's fine," he said. *"Can I get a ride to the bus stop?"*

My impulse to send him down the road was fading. I had the money; I just didn't have it there. He passed the tests; I would have to go home and get my checkbook.

"Sure, but you'll have to come with me to my apartment."

I hadn't been pastor for long. We still lived in our two-bedroom apartment at Kibbey Plaza, a short drive from the church and on the way to the bus stop, which, at the time, was the parking lot of the State Liquor Store on Seventh Street.

We went out to my electric-blue 1978 Honda Accord and headed for my place. Turning left onto Durston, I had to ask, *"So ... why are you dressed like that?"*

"I was over here applying for a job at a hotel."

"Oh. Are you from Butte, then?"

"No. That's where my treatment is; it's scheduled for today and I need to get back."

When you hear *treatment*, what do you think of? He looked neither sick nor weak. He seemed to be in good spirits; I even kind of liked the guy. As unusual as this situation was, he seemed very normal. The only "treatment" I could think of was drugs or alcohol or cancer. He looked too healthy for cancer.

"Treatment? For what? Anything serious?"

"AIDS. I have AIDS."

"AIDS?" I felt my foot lift off the pedal and my shoulder hit the glass of the door window as I unconsciously tried to separate myself from him. I was looking at him, probably like he was an alien.

He took it kindly, *"Yes. The only place there is treatment is in Butte."*

"Huh."

AIDS was still mysterious then, and I had never before been that close to anyone with it. I didn't know what to say. I was nervous, maybe scared. I was scared. Adding to this encounter the fact this man had AIDS and he was sitting in my car on the way to my apartment, the bizarre-o-meter in my head shattered.

I pulled into our assigned parking space at Kibbey. Cheryl was home with Madison who wasn't quite two. I couldn't take him up there.

I know this sounds hopelessly backward, but I was fearful to invite an AIDS patient into our apartment. I was worried about my wife and my daughter.

"Wait here. I'll be right back."

"Ok."

I turned the car off and took the keys. We lived on the second floor and I took the stairs two-at-a-time.

"You won't believe this," I said breathlessly, crashing through the door. *"There's a black guy with AIDS in the Honda who needs to get to Butte."*

"Excuse me?" Cheryl said.

"A black guy. He knocked on my office window wanting a ticket to Butte. I didn't have any money there so I brought him back here; on the way over, he told me he has AIDS. Where's the checkbook?"

I washed my hands. I know. I wish I could say I was more enlightened in 1995, but I wasn't.

"The checkbook's over there," Cheryl pointed to the desk in the living room.

I grabbed it and thought about what to do. There weren't a lot of options, but I was nervous. Should I call someone? The bus stop was close enough to walk to; should I tell him to walk over?

I had been taken by so many people wanting so many things. My imagination ran wild thinking of how I could now contract a deadly disease from one of them.

Something grabbed me from within and calmed me. This was my chance to do exactly what I said I wanted to: *Care. Help.*

I had given hundreds to charity-predators, and now I was thinking of hedging on someone who actually needed a hand? I had literally locked all the doors to His house, and God, as the saying goes, opened a window.

Or rather, He had a short, African-American man in a bow tie with AIDS needing to get to Butte tap on it. I feared what would happen to me if I refused this moment.

Walking down the stairs, I wondered if he'd still be there and if I'd get in the car. He was, and taking a deep breath and courage from prayer, I did.

Whatever made me get in that car saved me from the gimbal lock of The Last Compassion. I believe that, had I not, I would have irretrievably lost the dimension of life that makes it worth living.

A black man with AIDS in my Honda needing to get to Butte salvaged my compassion and kept alive the human warmth that has sustained me on two continents.

I sat with that kid on my lap in Africa until the sun set. Soon, he didn't have to hold my arm to his chest; I held it there and maybe even squeezed it a little tighter. This wasn't my first encounter with AIDS.

I got in the car outside my apartment, and my visitor smiled. We drove over to the bus stop and I went inside to get a ticket to Butte: $18, just like he said.

I walked out and handed it to him, *"Here you go. Good luck with your treatment."*

"Thanks. Thanks so much."

His dingy bus pulled into the equally dingy, litter-strewn parking lot, and I started to walk away.

I stopped.

"By the way, my name is Steve," I held out my hand.

He grabbed it firmly, *"Thank you, Steve."*

I smiled thinly, nodded, and left; I never saw him again. Knowing what AIDS does, I know there is little hope he is alive today.

But I also know the Lord used this man and this encounter in a way I wouldn't recognize for almost ten years. I may have helped him get to his treatment for a devastating physical disease, but it turns out he was my treatment for a devastating spiritual one: The Last Compassion.

The Replacement

I remember the clamoring sound of about 40 people milling about in the large main room designated as the auditorium of the rented storefront building used as a church. On a Montana January morning, every time someone opened the glass doors to come in, the ceiling furnace kicked on in a futile attempt to chase the creeping cold from the room.

An elderly lady on the foot-tall platform began to bang out some hymns on the vintage upright piano. It sounded like a solemn carnival. Welcome was in the air, and I found a seat in the metal folding chairs about halfway between the back and the platform.

I had never been to a church like this before.

When the preaching began, I initially thought I had walked into a cult. The minister paced back and forth. His voice raised and lowered passionately; he spit frequently. I think he may have cried. He even asked people to "come forward" to deal with what God was doing in their lives.

I don't remember the words of the sermon; I only remember how much they resonated in my soul.

As a young Christian, I had finally found a place where a young pastor preached the Bible with enthusiasm and genuine conviction. My eyes must have been the size of peaches from realizing I found my home.

I was eighteen and had just made an inadvisable move from Lincoln, Nebraska, to Bozeman, Montana, in the middle of an unforgiving winter. In this church, however, I began to consider the possibility that this was why I had come: to find this cluster of believers.

I dove headlong into the ministry, and I loved it. I couldn't believe that church could be so enjoyable. Every Sunday it seemed we made strides in attendance, giving, in community. I looked forward to every service, and each one ended too soon.

The preacher was a master at his calling; I could listen to him expound for hours. We loved him, and he loved his church. Together, we were making a splash in a town where many churches had gone to die.

We purchased land; we had plans drawn up; we increased in attendance. Eighty people packed into that storefront each Sunday, and all the saints dwelt in peace. Under the influence of this congregation and the passion and enthusiasm of our preacher, I began to sense a call to the ministry and set plans to go to college.

By the time I left for my Bible college adventures eighteen months later, our church had gone from about forty people on a good Sunday to about one hundred on an average one. Leaving it behind, my memories were of sweet fellowship, outstanding preaching, and a congregation with a mandate.

I would never find it again.

While I was in Missouri, the church grew even more. It was bulging at the seams, with people standing in the back. Staff was hired. Families were added nearly every Sunday. The building started to go up, and people kept coming.

At the dedication of the new building, over 200 people attended. Seven years after the church was born, there was a sparkling picture of a sparkling staff standing in front of a new sparkling white facility.

All of which signified the beginning of the end.

Actually, the end began before this, but this is where it began to show. What hadn't shown for years were issues in our pastor's personal life—the kinds of issues that rise like a creeping vine to slowly choke off dreams.

On a deceptively ordinary Sunday afternoon while in college, I got a phone call from a friend in the church; she was crying. She read me the text of the resignation from the founding pastor. Our pastor. My pastor. It was over. His last Sunday was only two weeks away.

I skipped a day or two of classes to return for his last Sunday in September with a friend of mine who had also been part of FBC. The building I had only known as a drawing had been completed in my absence, and I sat in the auditorium for the first time watching what I thought would never happen: Our pastor leaving our church. And he was not just leaving our church, but leaving the ministry.

He preached from Paul's encounter with the Ephesian elders and, like Paul, commended us to God. I sat in my pew, hearing his words but replaying the innocence of better times. As the clock ticked down on the last sermon, I realized how much of my life had been molded by this man, his ministry, and the church he founded.

When he finished, the sound of sobbing was everywhere; the church seemed collectively inconsolable. We each took our turn at the door saying goodbye to the only preacher many of us had ever known. This didn't feel right. It felt like something out of time, something thirty years too soon.

I wept like a mourner at a funeral. The following day, I went back to Springfield, and he left Bozeman.

Several years later, after an excruciating eighteen-month interim, the church he started called me to be their third pastor. The building had lost its sparkle, and the congregation had dwindled into a shell of its old self.

We had about 65 survivors of a nuclear-sized ecclesiastical disaster and a trunk of memories that haunted us. Chief among the ghosts that tormented my memory was the last conversation I had had with my pastor before assuming the pastorate of the church he founded.

The week the church asked me to be a candidate for pastor, he called and told me he had made a mistake. He told me his marriage was in trouble, and he felt it all went back to leaving this church. He said he was connected to this church and, if I would step aside, we could see a miracle happen. He would come back and, by doing so, precious things in his life could be restored. We could pick back up where things had been left and get back to where we were supposed to be.

He asked me to consider it and call him back.

There was nothing in the world I wanted more; I was twenty-eight and still believed in happy endings. I sought counsel from many people to determine if this was possible. I asked a mutual pastor friend; I asked our former associate who had grown up with him; I asked a member of our church who was like a father to him. They were unanimous: Impossible.

I couldn't bear to call him back and tell him. I was young, only two years out of college and only three years from his resignation. I couldn't bear the thought of telling him no, so I didn't.

I accepted the call of the church he started without calling him back, and I think he resented that for some time. It's been unsettling to live with over the last ten years.

Life went on, our church survived, we grew. We're back to about where he left it; we've built our own buildings. We enjoy church again. I still miss the "old church," but I'm glad we're at a place where people are excited about "our church."

I still miss him.

The last time I saw my pastor was in 1993—until this day.

Ten years after I last saw him and nearly eighteen years to the day that I first discovered this church, he walked into his old office about 9 a.m. and left four hours later. We talked, reminisced, and asked questions of each other.

He wore remorse on his sleeve as he spoke of the few things that had been going well. He spoke of regret. I spoke of memories. He revealed his struggles. I revealed my disappointments. He told me about how much he has suffered in twelve years. He seemed humbled, sad, in a resigned sort of way, and genuinely trying to salvage his life.

I sat there looking at him from behind the desk in the study he first occupied. I said, *"This feels weird to me; I should be on that side of the desk talking to you."*

It did, too. Even though I have been pastor here two years longer than he was, I felt weird—awkward—in the role reversal.

In his eyes, I could still see the love he has for the only church he ever pastored—almost like a lost, innocent love. But what he said next floored me.

He looked at me and said, *"Let me tell you what I think happened here. It is a parallel to when Samuel informed Saul that 'The Lord hath rent the kingdom from you and given it to one that is better than thou.'"*

He said he now understood that I was brought here for this. God knew his struggles would catch up with him, he said, and the church would need another. He said I was that "other."

The scenario surprised me; I had never considered it. In the dizzying sadness of losing a beloved pastor and in the swale of a ministry struggling to find its feet after a near-knockout punch,

God was crafting something new and preparing another. In the sad notes of the moments I had endured to get here, I lost track of the Composer's symphony.

Could people have apprehended the anointing of David while Saul was on the throne? Could Barnabas have known Paul would rise to prominence as he journeyed to bring the outcast to Antioch? People who feel like they are drowning so rarely see the shore in front of them.

In the wake of our conversation, I revisited the fact that we aren't able to know the purposes and destinies God is leading us to as we desperately fight off discouragement. This may be the most hopeful truth I have ever discovered, because it reminds me that the struggle and confusion of the moment is no indication that God has stopped crafting joyful things to come.

God is always working toward His expected end. Listening to my old pastor that morning, I understood again that it is the nature of God to compose the grand symphony of our joy from the saddest notes we collect over the course of life.

Government Cheese

Don't we all have sad stories?

Sadness and tragedy seem to come in a variety pack of shapes and sizes, customizable to every life. One man's sadness is another man's relief, and what to one would be incredible poverty is to another incredible wealth.

If we all sat down together, I suppose everyone could testify of events in our life that have brought us to the brink of unstoppable tears and unspeakable despair. Maybe there would only be rare instances over the course of a charmed life, but, the last I checked, sadness is hard to measure relatively.

Which is why I normally avoid the "Oliver Twist" moments of my less-than-charmed life. When I think of them, I tend to immediately consider other people and their almost certainly more emotionally devastating stories. It's ... embarrassing ... to me to think of my life as "sad," not in a prideful way, but in a deferent way: I can't escape feeling that claiming my sad stories as actual sadness is insulting to genuine sadness.

Consequently, I have generally laughed at the events of my life that some might consider tragic. In a different sort of sad way, I suppose that laughter has been a way of coping with the incidents I desperately didn't want to be sad.

I was twelve when we were left on our own—and by "we" I mean my sister, my mom, and me. Our sole income at that time was my mom's $1,000 a month secretary's salary. In 1978, $1,000 a month was rich enough not to be eligible for standard Welfare but poor enough to really need it.

In fact, the worst blow to our survival as a broken family was when bouncing checks became illegal; not that my mom intended to bounce them, just that she hoped to "float" them. For about six months.

When the consequences of that strategy became painful enough to stop doing it, my mom turned to more conventional methods of providing for us. In the early eighties, government surplus food was released for distribution to the public; I know nothing of the details of it nor even how my mom came to learn about it. What I remember is her coming home with boxes of powdered milk and Government Cheese.

The "powdered milk" could only be taken for milk by someone who had never tasted actual milk; it was more like milk-colored water. If you tried to have it with cereal, you might as well have drenched your Rice Krispies in water.

Unless of course, you discovered bugs in your bowl, whereupon you swore the stuff off forever after garping up what you had already eaten. Which I did.

The cheese, on the other hand, was different. Insects couldn't hide in it, because the rectangular bricks seemed to have the density of a neutron star. It had a wonderfully artificial yellow color and tasted like "Velveeta" with a hint of New Jersey dust.

The bricks came in stark, white plastic wrappers on which was written plainly but appropriately, "CHEESE," in black, all-capped letters. No ingredients were listed that I can remember, probably because it was about one molecule short of being plastic and barely fit for human consumption. I imagine there are some people born around 1995 with two thumbs on each hand whose genetic anomaly can be traced directly to the Government Cheese their parents consumed as kids.

And, yet, we liked it. Which is fortunate, because Government Cheese was a staple in our home for several years.

I don't know who the federal genius was who first thought that processed cheese would be something the nation must have in times of crisis, but he saved our Government Bacon more than once. I wonder how that conversation might have gone...

"Well, Mr. Senator, if the pinko Rooskies start lobbing Nucular warheads over Santa's workshop like snowballs on a playground, we believe one of the things we'll need to ensure our survival as a culture is ... is American Cheese... Each brick'll have the density of a neutron star and we can store them in bunkers throughout the US. One brick can feed the state of Indiana for a month."

However it went, he couldn't have known back in the days when artificial cheese must surely have seemed like the zenith of human ingenuity that scores of American families (including mine) would be sustained by his foresight. In some strange, strange, Dr. Strangelove sort of way, I owe that man a thank you.

To this point in my adulthood, I have never had to feed my kids Government Cheese, if there's any of it left. I have been pretty proud of that until an episode this week hit me like a glass of cold water in a hot shower.

Rumor had it back in 2006 that the world was going to end in '08 or '09. Montana has always been a kind of zoo for lunatics, and this last rumored end of the world brought some in our church into close contact with a millionaire who actually believed this timeline of the Apocalypse.

So, this particular millionaire loaded up for the end of the world by buying a house in a secluded area of secluded Montana, complete with massive underground bunker not far off. The house was pretty ordinary, but the bunker was a different story.

It held 4 brand new RVs and a new truck along with living quarters for 3 separate families. Apparently, the RVs were for the families to go find a nice quiet place out in the irradiated Nuclear Winter to camp when they got on each other's nerves.

Along with these essentials were more conventional staples: food, cleaning supplies, first-aid assortments. When people think of "survival" food, I think most everyone thinks of wheat. But, seriously, what do you do with wheat? If I had a metric ton of wheat, I would starve to death. And so would most everyone else.

Which explains why *this* bunker was stocked with survival items like Mandarin oranges, M&Ms, olive oil, coffee, Grey Poupon, barbecue sauce, meats of all varieties, jugs of aspirin and Lysol, and, at one time, two million dollars in gold bars. After all, why survive the holocaust of humanity if you can't enjoy some Mandarin oranges and a good cup of coffee afterward?

And the quantities of these items were measured not by the case, but by the pallet. Literally tons of food and supplies to last several half-lives were warehoused below ground. When it was happening, all of us just shook our heads at the incredible waste and suckerdom of people cash-rich and sense-poor.

Alas, the world remains, the millionaire moved back to Florida, and now needs to unload her survivalist paradise in Southwest Montana. She entrusted the dispersal of her accumulated survival food cache to someone in our church.

Wanting to make it available to some of the more hurting in our congregation, they brought a fraction of it back the other day. We unloaded the items onto folding tables in our church building and thought of whom to call. Six families seemed obvious to everyone.

Something very sobering about this economic crash became very clear and very sobering when everyone agreed these particular families were in undeniable need: Each one of them—only a couple years ago—were making hundreds of thousands of dollars. Now, they are people looking at empty cupboards in million dollar homes that no one wants, even at a fraction of their cost.

While not in that particular situation, we were given our share as well, being people who are making less than what they used to and needing their money to go as far as possible. I loaded up our boxes, staring at the food I didn't buy, noting some of it had passed its expiration date.

A little of my previous pride died a quiet death.

As I continued walking out to our truck with more boxes, I thought of ... Government Cheese. This wasn't Government Cheese, but the idea seemed to be the same. My pride was now dying a very angry death.

As self-pity and pride were about to collide in their own fissionable way, I considered something else. I remembered the chuckles and sneers we all enjoyed when the survivalist millionaire purchased all these "essentials," and I wondered if behind it all wasn't so much the paranoia of the colossally gullible but, rather, the providential hand of God.

The questions kept coming: Might it be possible that God was behind all the apparent lunacy several years ago because He knew what was about to befall all of us who believed we had everything under control? Was it possible God had been providing for our needs years before we became victims of a time none of us could see coming? Does God use the outlandish theories of tea-leaf readers and the extravagance of the overfunded to provide for His people?

Is God *that* providential? Yes, I concluded. He is.

And whether it's endless pallets of unused contemporary survival food or a bag full of Government Cheese, I owe someone a thank you that my pride wars against. Not so much to the guy who thought laying up cubic miles of processed cheese would be a good idea nor even so much to all those who go on pointless spending sprees to survive the destruction of humanity ...

but to the Father, Whose wisdom, grace, and providence looks after all the fools who think that because they no longer feast on Government Cheese, they will never need a little help.

Seriously

I wish it were more spiritual. Even, I wish it were more selfless.

I stood on this late Saturday night in the parking lot, taking in the lights flashing blue-white-red-blue-white-red and watched the smoke ooze up over the roof with a menacing determination. If the building had been 100 stories taller, it could have been the World Trade Center on September 11, 2001.

It wasn't. It was Heritage Christian School in August, 2012. It was where I had watched countless events involving my kids, from sports to singing to graduation last May. It is where so much of my life had happened in the last ten years.

And it was on fire.

It is also where Fellowship Baptist Church landed as a layover on our now eight-year building program that had seen more than its share of postponements and disappointments and emergencies of cash and congregation. We sold our building eighteen months earlier in anticipation of soon building, but as costs climbed unexpectedly, we were forced to stay in this gym longer than we anticipated.

When we began our Building Program, we were a healthy-appearing church in terms of attendance and finances, a church with a staff of four and with its own building it had occupied for twenty years. This Saturday night, in this parking lot, we were a church that had lost sizable percentages of people and money, had sold its building of twenty years, had plans to say goodbye to its sole remaining staff member in the morning, and had placed much of its essential equipment and future ability to meet in that gym.

And it was on fire.

The thought I had as I watched wasn't a Bible verse or inspirational quote and it wasn't even concerned with the school itself. I simply looked up and took the whole scene in and said to myself, *"Seriously?"*

It's not the stuff of inspiration, to be sure. I hope it doesn't wind up being the title of my biography, but it seemed to be the only response I had left after all the troughs and tragedies of the last near-decade.

The spectacle had crossed the timeline from very late Saturday night to very early Sunday morning. In the dizziness of the event, I tried to account for everything that needed to be addressed before the sun rose on our routine service schedule: *"Where would our church meet? ... Would we meet? ... How do we get the word out? ... What would I say? ... What next?"*

Over phone lines and across the Internet, we let everyone know we would meet in my front yard. It was our only option.

People brought their lawn chairs and the food they were planning to bring to the send-off for our Associate Pastor, Jon, and his family. We sent people over to the charred remains to redirect people who hadn't gotten word, and we arranged for the kids to meet at the members' house catty-corner from us.

I retreated to a room in our home where I abandoned my entire morning's plan. After all we had been through and all the goals we had hoped were imminent, after so many years and so many promises, I genuinely wasn't sure what to expect from this church I pastor.

Honestly, I wasn't sure what to expect from me either.

In addition to being one of the most challenging (read: "worst") summers of my life, the erosion of our situation mocked me. We had sold our building on promise of constructing a new one, and now we were meeting in my yard. I had gone from the confident leader of a major ecclesiastical venture in the form of a 30,000 square foot construction project, costing millions of dollars to a now-exhausted guy, whose only response to the latest challenge was, *"Seriously?"*

As the time approached to start our improvised service, I watched the people intently to gauge their spirit. On a normal Sunday, our church, like many others, has a "buzz" and a busyness to them that resembles the floor of the great Stock Exchanges of the world: musicians and singers practicing, volunteers setting up spaces, teachers making copies and kids running everywhere.

If you stood in our foyer the week before, you would have watched people passing each other in a sterile hallway with a cup of coffee in their hand, giving a glancing, obligatory smile as they did. You could have listened as the usual clusters of individuals talked superficially about nothing of importance.

We were different on this morning. On so many Sunday mornings, we are just individual pieces of a moving machine; on this morning, we were one. We didn't have the swagger of individuals and we weren't thinking in consumer terms. The bulwarks of individuality were reduced to ash by the fire and on my lawn was gathered something remarkable: a congregation.

Many home Bible studies have more planning behind them than did this particular Sunday's service. We sang one song; we had no instruments, no video projection, and no hymnals.

We only remembered to take an offering after the service was finished.

Without the instruments and walls, I listened to the stripped down, unplugged words of "Amazing Grace," chosen in no small part because it is a song everyone knows—it needs no words projected on a screen or typed on a page. The old hymn is a dependable balm that draws souls heavenward when the world has done all it can to drain joy from our lives. It was the only song that made sense on this morning.

When I stood to preach, a neighbor was watching from across the street, and more than once people strolled by walking a dog or getting a little exercise. Before me was assembled people who appeared to be expecting a barbecue or a game of badminton; they were in assorted lawn furniture and on blankets and huddled under trees; they were wearing sunglasses; some had dressed for church, others for a morning on the lawn.

But they were all there.

I settled on the only thing that made sense to me that morning. I preached from Acts 8 and the great persecution in Jerusalem that scattered Christians to the wind. I pointed out how God uses means we wouldn't invite into our lives to accomplish His goal of dislodging people from their complacency in order to focus them on His calling in their life.

Because God is good and perfect, we know that a great persecution was exactly what the church in Jerusalem needed at the time. I told the people this led me to conclude that God looked at our church after years of plodding, hoping, giving, believing, and expecting and determined the best thing to do for us Saturday, August 25th, 2012 was have the place we were meeting in destroyed by arson, melting down all our equipment in the process.

It's so often true that we want the gain without the pain, and like our ancient brethren in Acts, we would never have invited this into our lives. I reminded people that the pain we experience in times like this is not incidental to the plan—the pain *is* the plan.

Putting us out on the street right now is not something that just happened. It is what God willed to happen; it is what God knows is the best thing to happen.

We prayed at the end. All of us. With one voice. I could hear whispers of requests and muffled "amens" of agreement; for my part, I contributed to the sound of weeping. It was a symphony of emotion lifted up and presented to God as a confident offering of thanks for His presence and purpose. It was ... inspiring ... comforting ... assuring.

I lifted my head from prayer and looked out at this gathering of God's people on my front lawn. Later, I pondered how we had gathered without media, music, schedules, organization, or a building. I wish I could say we had nobly gathered to defy the evil that burns schools and displaces churches or that we had courageously gathered to honor the Lord Whose worship cannot be held hostage by the impulses of wicked people.

But I can't. The truth is that we gathered because that's what churches do.

This service on the green showed me something precious. Church buildings, church projects, and church possessions can be eaten up by moth, rust, and fire, but the *church*—the people—remains.

Looking for a new place to meet, we have taken offerings in refrigerator crisper trays, we have played music around a table because our music stands were lost, we bring sunscreen to worship because we have no roof. And yet, we gather.

We gather with a large spirit and inexplicable smile while we talk a little longer. We gather and we pray more thankfully, sing more thoughtfully. We gather and we anticipate more, because God has once again made Himself the architect of our future.

I often face the disappointments and confusion in my life the same way I faced this devastation in our church, but the lesson is the same. A month ago, if someone would have said the next best step for our church would be to have all its "necessities" destroyed by fire and to be without a building to meet in for several weeks or a month or more, I think I would have had one response: *"Seriously?"*

Yes. Seriously.

CHAPTER 6

....

RENEWAL & LOVE

The Spirit of a Boy

I'm told that spring is here. I wouldn't know it first hand, because winter refuses to leave Montana until the last snowflake dies fighting beneath June's unstoppable sun.

Yes, June.

So my dreams of spring consist solely of memories, images of a place I couldn't wait to leave when I was a boy. While so many others are swinging golf clubs and oiling bikes, preparing to enjoy the newfound warmth of a fresh season, I am left to my "virtual" spring in a time and culture under-appreciated while I strolled through them both.

Maybe at thirty-seven I am beginning to appreciate things about life I once thought of as disposable and mundane. The people I once considered expendable now find a little corner of warmth in my heart; places I once deemed insufferable are finding an audience in my spirit for their calls to come "home."

Spring is a season that awakens all these memories and stirs what is becoming an almost unquenchable desire to rediscover the simplicity of a younger, if not simpler time.

Now on the low end of middle age, I am also beginning to understand how far I am from home. Not that I do not consider Montana home, just that it's not. You understand this if younger days carried you along a trail leading away from where you were raised.

Every good reason sent us away; some, like myself, swore they would never return. Yet, as life's pages turn, I find those disposables and mundanities are the missing pieces that have left behind a persistent hole in my being.

I am a long way from home.

I am a long way from Jerry Myers whose phone number I still know from my boyhood. I dialed 4**-4034 so many times that, nearly thirty years after I last did, it seems possible to pick up the phone today, call 1974, and ask if Jerry could come out and play.

At this stage in my life, with a church, a staff, a wife, three kids, a dog, and a mortgage, I'm not sure I remember how to play. But there are two things that continually encourage me to renew my playing credentials: A season and a son.

Spring is a friend. It doesn't demand that you sacrifice the focus of your life in order to revel in its gifts—like the first patch of dry dirt behind the house or next to the driveway that invited me to a battlefield fought with plastic soldiers and plastic tanks.

When you are a boy, time is invested in important things you imagine adults consider a waste. But men envy boys they see "wasting" time on a pile of dirt or mountain of rocks or fields of mud, because they know that those days, which they once longed to see melt beneath adulthood, are gone.

If someone caught a man taking an afternoon to set up a colossal battle on a fine stretch of dirt with plastic soldiers and pretend generals, they would wonder about his maturity or responsibility—maybe even his sanity. A boy, on the other hand, can kneel down and fire away at evil or drive over the obstacles with dump trucks, carry the hour, seize the day, save the world, and be home in time for dinner.

I think men love having sons in no small part so they can pass on the truly important matters they have gleaned from life. Not so much the lessons from careers, accolades, or even education, but from boyhood.

There is a selfish element even to this. Most men face a reality of complexities and disappointments, brimming with deadlines and demands, heartaches and confrontation. Our boys give us an excuse to leave that world for a time and recreate one where everything goes according to our own sovereign, idealistic imagination, like we did when we were too young to know ideals die.

Over time, I've come to believe that the best of men carry with them an echo of the boy they once were throughout life. Every boy can't wait to be a man, but, as life plods forward and the years blur into decades, that man begins to see with new clarity and longing appreciation everything that was good about his boyhood. The son at his side gives him an excuse to visit that place again.

Down the hill from my house, the field adjoining Nebraska Ag-Products provided the rare, luxurious, wide-open space in a city necessary to launch kites. Into a sky that rained the color blue down in drenching showers of warmth, swarms of people gathered for this ritual of no redeeming value except that it was fun. And outside.

The kites slide up to a clear spring sky tethered by a bowed string and anchored to a boy gazing upward. He wonders if he can get it a foot or two higher; he wonders what the view is like. He thinks the pride he feels must be what the Wright brothers sensed when their contraption defied gravity.

In spring, this kite is his spirit, and both soar higher into the welcoming sky than seems safe. But nothing seems more right.

Today, that field where I once ran is gone; apartments now sit where neighborhood kids escaped narrow streets and power lines that mock kites. Yet, the sky, the boy inside, and the season carry on; every year, the dance is renewed. Kites are dug out of winter's clutter, and armies of former boys grip the miniature hands of men in their making and stroll to the middle of fields that will one day most likely be occupied with the dreams of developers.

Together, they launch a piece of plastic tethered by string into a sky that rains blue down upon them like water from a refreshing falls. Dad has been here before; this sky is an old friend.

Here—now—he remembers that dreams are not so much fulfilled as they are renewed. The boy beside him is getting his first lessons in a truth he'll learn across the days of life: As the years march relentlessly on, the best things are usually the ones left behind in days we couldn't wait to get past.

Somewhere out there this spring is a kite untethered, free to sail upward and explore the spring sky. Holding on as it ascends into the endless azure brilliance is the spirit of a boy which the man he'll become will never outgrow.

The Last Train Out of Disaster

"I'm trying to be … prudent … From here, I can see how the end could come."

This is what I told our church leadership about two weeks ago. I told them that my dear wife of nineteen years and I needed some time away, especially with a seminal building project about to swing into full force. Two and a half to three weeks would be nice.

They looked worried.

August is an abyss for church work, I've noticed. As people recklessly snarf up the last few weeks of the last month that promises to be warm in Montana, Sunday attendance dwindles in numbers. This August, my sanity was also dwindling.

It has been ten years since I have taken a vacation lasting more than 48 hours that didn't involve meetings, preaching somewhere to pay for it, or staying with relatives in exotic places like Primghar, Iowa, or Denton, Nebraska. With several capable staff members, I wouldn't be missed.

The church generously supplied the money and shipped me and Cheryl off to any destination we wanted. Which is nice, because we didn't really have a destination in mind. Just a journey.

It began at a train station in Whitefish, Montana.

Whitefish is a small, alpine town just beneath Big Mountain Ski Resort. Most of the buildings are capped with metal roofs, giving gleaming witness to the amount of winter snow that falls on them.

We drove north to the Whitefish station on a day when the earth seemed to have no roof and the sky's blue had been drained out by the sheer brilliance of the sun. Montana is rarely hot, per se, but the sun is intense. When it is unabated by clouds, you begin to understand how french fries feel under the heat lamps—you feel "cooked" more than "hot."

Our 1990 Suburban had no working air conditioner, so the hot, dry wind blew on us the entire 350 miles to Whitefish. My arm still has a carpet burn sensation from hanging out the window.

We clutched tickets for train 27—The Empire Builder.

In its heyday, the Builder was the pride of the Great Northern Railway and highballed from Chicago, slicing through Minnesota into the grain-infested wasteland of North Dakota, across the "highline" of Montana and over the Cascades to Seattle. Amtrak's version splits in Spokane, with one portion continuing across former GN trackage to Seattle and another section traversing old Spokane, Portland, and Seattle tracks to Portland.

Our tickets were for one sleeper car to Portland.

My grandpa was a railroad depot agent in Gretna, Nebraska, among other towns; my love for trains predates my birth and is as inexplicable as it was unavoidable. On still, heavy summer evenings of my ever-sweetening childhood, he would lay in bed with me and turn on the vintage 1930s floor radio, which stood four feet if it stood an inch.

Watching the glow from the dial bathe the room in a warm yellow as KFAB's Omaha signal squealed in and out of tune, we talked about what we'd do tomorrow and what he did decades ago. When the lonely horn of the San Francisco Zephyr stirred the evening air of Gretna, it was time for a kid to sleep.

The Empire Builder stirred the evening air of Whitefish. Cheryl and I watched the headlight of the engine flow into the station amidst the clanking of bells from under the carriage. We stood on the platform like people with no other purpose than to leave.

Our sleeper was on the upper deck of the last car of the train—a Superliner. Room C had a couch that folded out into a bed and an upper berth that folded down. Across from the couch was a chair, which was perfect for reading or watching the scenery through the large picture window. We also had our own toilet and shower, a true luxury on a train.

We settled into the room and waited for the Builder to jolt forward into the setting sun. No jolt, only a smooth glide that started us down the track. The train leaves Whitefish at 9:16 pm, leaving little time for scenery before being swallowed up by the night.

There was time, however, for me and Cheryl to sit and stare at each other—me with a goofy smile on my face for being on a train and her with a goofy smile on her face for the goofy smile on my face. We both were trying desperately to leave the concerns and stresses that had risen dangerously unchecked in our life back on the platform.

Trains have a movement all their own; it is the movement of escape. It's a good movement—rocking, gentle swaying, all choreographed to the sound of life being left behind. The evening deepened across the rugged northwestern corner of Montana.

On the train, it was too late to eat, and many of the passengers were settling into a night's sleep. We sat across from each other quietly. Still smiling. For the first time in too long, we had nowhere to be and no time but our own and no particular place to go.

We breathed deeply, trying to exhale the recent stresses from our spirit. We breathed like people who caught the last train out of a doomed town, only ours was a doomed lifestyle that was careening far too quickly toward a future of regret and a labyrinth of "what ifs?"

We had escaped the doom into the unwritten night of a journey too long not taken. Only, the journey lay ahead; this moment was for us. Not many times will life allow people a timeout. When the precious ones come along, people are wise to seize them without apology.

As Portland rose up on the edge of America to greet us, we were remembering something so many lose over the course of being married and living life: we remembered we liked each other. We remembered we began our story as a husband and a wife, not business partners contractually bound to raise kids and satisfy others.

The Empire Builder was the last train out of disaster because, for a precious few hours, we were insulated from the things we loved that were killing us. Finally free from the temptation to ignore ourselves, we found a couple of people we hadn't realized we missed so much: us.

August in My Memory

I think most people with small towns lurking in their past revisit them more frequently as they age, even if it's only in their memory. I think it's especially true if that small town was where a grandparent seemed to always be waiting, ever glad to have their grandkid as a sidekick for a few days.

People think Montana is cold. I suppose the assumption is that igloos dot the landscape 50 out of 52 weeks of the year and that we who live here are always struggling to keep from succumbing to frostbite. There's an old saying, *"There are three months of the year in Montana: July, August, and Winter."*

Most likely, this was originally said by someone who lived in Southern California all their life.

Montana summers have at least a week or two with temperatures normally only found on the surface of the sun. Or, at least, that's how it feels. Air conditioners frequently sell out by late July when the holdouts who defiantly refused to give in to an eighty-five degree house on the Fourth of July scoop up the leftovers from Walmart, hoping to finally fall asleep before midnight.

Summer winds shove smoke into our valley from whatever forest is currently on fire, veiling the mountains we took for granted in spring behind a weak, brownish smear. Many people discover too late that the direct Montana sun can raise blisters on unprotected skin in a couple of hours.

Montana summers are also quite arid. In the absence of any humidity at all, the intensity of the sun and the hazy brown horizon make the sky seem like tinfoil wrapped over a turkey roasting in an oven. You're the turkey.

Sitting here on this bright August Saturday afternoon marred slightly by the smoky haze from fires in Canada, I'm irresistibly drawn to times when Saturdays were different. Now, Saturdays are about getting everything ready for the next day. For me, Saturday has been a deadline for years.

But I'm remembering when it was a welcome break from the previous five days and was the centerpiece of the weekend. Saturday meant I was free from classes or, if it was summer, that grown-ups would crowd the pool we ruled throughout the week.

For some reason, I can't help but think back to a small, thoughtless town in Southeast Nebraska where my family has its roots. My small town is Gretna, Nebraska. It's where my grandparents raised my parents, and, growing up, there was nowhere I'd rather be on any day of the week.

August Saturdays there were long and scorched with oppressive heat. Nebraska is hot and humid all summer long, and the only people complaining about it in August are those who either don't know how to start a conversation or end one.

In 1972, it is a slow life in rural America that doesn't yet know that time has breezed by like an uninterested stranger on the street. Beyond the cornfield borders of the town, society is building an America that will no longer be in need of communities this size.

Urban centers of commerce replace the "uptowns" of rural communities. New generations will spruce these towns up like antique trucks, scraping off the rust of yesteryear, painting over the deteriorating bond of community, and putting on just enough new chrome to make the place shiny.

But they really only want to sleep here; there is no interest in mending the fabric of an actual town. As I've seen it today, it's more like living in an amusement park where developers construct the facade of an era without the bonds between people and place that made the era so appealing in the first place.

In the summers of my youth, when Gretna was more than a safe sleeping distance from Omaha, the trademarks of August were days that slid slowly by and nights that hung thick in the air. I am six, maybe seven, as I look around in my memory.

The Saturdays I remember feel more like a place than a time, like I could just drive there. It calls in such a way that I almost believe it could be resurrected from the heap of unappreciated days lying in my past.

Canvassing my memory are August Saturdays when my grandpa and I went to work in the morning down to the aging depot that had stood watch over the mainline of the CB&Q railroad for decades. Here, I explored dusty freight areas and passenger waiting rooms sitting obsolete in the exhaust of commercial airline travel.

My playground was boxcars on sidetracks. I climbed in the massive, steel rolling stock with faded paint schemes of once-mighty railroads merged into oblivion. When afternoons baked beneath a canopy of heat that seemed to melt the dirt, I had nothing to do but go out onto the tracks and pretend I was moving imaginary trains in between watching real ones blast past.

And that's how I remember them. I remember afternoons of incredible quiet in a town that didn't know how to be loud. The only break from the constant background buzz of nothing happening was the scheduled monstrous, crushing chaos of thousands of tons of freight gliding over steel rails through cornfields on the west side of town or around the bend into dark ravines to the east.

Lunch was lazy, and we drank coffee poured from a beat-up thermos that looked like bears had gnawed on it. In a room that once held crowds of people waiting for trains and all the chatter of expectant travel to places like Omaha or Minneapolis, we talked.

I wish I could remember what we talked about; I think I would give most any material possession I have to remember one conversation with my grandpa in that creaky old depot. Sometimes I can't help but think of all the opportunities I wasted not asking him questions. I always regret not listening more.

But I suppose that is what a grandson does. I suppose that is why he is so loved by a grandpa: he has no agenda. He's too young to disappoint him, too simple to fail him, too innocent to have outgrown him, and too happy to ask for money. A young boy loves being around an old man, and enjoying it is the extent of his responsibility.

I know I did. I know he knew I did.

We go home early because it's the weekend, and another thoughtless Saturday passes in this town. I have many more to spend in '72, and I don't realize the comfortable memory I am living.

It is quiet here. The civil defense siren—or "*whistle*," as it was more commonly called—blares its haunting wail at noon and six p.m. Air conditioners hum into the slightly receding heat of the afternoon and the day's light subtly changes color without dimming, announcing that the sun is thinking about setting soon.

Locusts call in the trees overhead, their wavy sound providing the soundtrack of the season. I hear the diminutive rumble of a lawn mower crank up and the sound of sprinklers splashing in the streets. The trees over my head give a kaleidoscope view of the heated, pale blue sky as their leaves twitch in a breeze no one can feel.

From where I stand, next to a light pole planted in the front yard next to the narrow concrete walk that leads to my grandpa's front door, I hear the purr of tires slowly driving down a brick boulevard canopied by stately elms and oaks. Further into the evening, the sharp "clank" of iron horseshoes being tossed in the abandoned lot uptown echoes down to me, and people begin emerging from the shelter of their freon palaces onto lazy chairs perched upon long porches to watch life for a while.

Everything is fine ... fine in a way it never will be again.

On this wilting, hazy Montana Saturday afternoon a long way—a long time—from my yesterdays, the Augusts of my memory call from beyond the desk and my deadline to remind me that the Saturdays of leisure may be over but they have also grown sweeter.

In fact, oddly, they may never have been closer to me than thirty years later. Maybe that's why we have memories. Maybe they are the assurance that anything happening today can be a sweet encouragement tomorrow.

Maybe they're just sweet.

Echoes of Who I Expected to Be

This is the wrong thing to do at the wrong time. It is late on a Saturday evening, I have a sermon due tomorrow at 11, and I have scarcely a paragraph written. It isn't the first time this has happened, but it never sits comfortably with me.

Tonight, the first night of 2005, I am interrupted by something that has been nagging at me for, literally, years. It's like white noise in my mind: something that is always there, reasonably harmless, extremely annoying. Worse, it portends of something bigger, more sinister.

Sinister, not in the Hannibal Lecter sense, but in the I-don't-want-to-face-this sense, sinister in the if-I-keep-busy-I-will- be-able-to-ignore-this sense. It's hard to describe what draws my attention away from the approaching deadline of Sunday morning.

They are, like, echoes, I guess, echoes of something I shouldn't have forgotten because it was me to begin with. The sense itself is harmless, but it feels like an imprint left over from a person no longer here.

When left alone, the echoes are little more than flirtatious distractions, often calling me to enjoy a short trip down Memory Lane. However, just as smoke blown through a room reveals invisible beams of light, certain things give these echoes definable features.

They take shape from either old things that conjure memories of who I once was or new things that remind me of a stranger I swore I would never forget. Being seized by the echoes is like waking up in the morning to the disturbing realization you don't remember what you look like.

Not recognizing ourselves in a mirror is abhorrent; our own appearance is too personal to forget. Forget your way, ok; forget your name, it happens. But we all know what we look like; we could all pick ourselves out of line-up.

Except when the echoes stir. When they do, it becomes difficult to identify the reflection, and a person stares back who looks, well, like the person you thought you'd be so many years ago.

Who was the person you expected to be back when skies rained down possibilities and the days stretched long into the horizon?

Past days aren't always good days. Sometimes, the best thing about them is that, back then, they were unwritten; they were unclaimed. Who were you planning on being when you were architecting your life, just before the construction began?

Most of the time, these days remain safe from serious contemplation. Their dreams of us rest lifeless on the heap of juvenile expectations after finally conceding life's insistence that they were formulated not knowing that what we dreamt couldn't be achieved.

Mercifully, the echoes usually remain just that—faint sounds of an idealist being muzzled by both maturity and reality, so called. The fading calls of these echoes normally do little more than bring a lightly creased, nostalgic smile to wiser adults as they hurry on toward the end of their life.

But every now and then, I've had the feeling that the echoes want to be so much more than mere nostalgia. On a night like this, they insist on having their say; they demand their time.

Those brave enough to pause and listen endure a wrenching reading of indictments chronicling our crimes against the humanity that matters most to us—our own. The echoes ignore your cries stipulating to them all and accepting whatever consequences come. They read on, undeterred by your confession and, holding your head up, forcing you to remember something. Someone.

They want you to remember you. To remember the you you planned on being, the you *you* wanted to be.

The you you are not.

Remember them? Remember the days before your
first position, before your first discussion about your future?
Remember long contemplations of how you would win the world,
solve the problems, carry the day, and get the girl? Remember the
idealism that came standard with every sunrise?

I read a story not long ago about a running joke General
Electric engineers had amongst themselves. Since they were
invented, the filament in light bulbs produced a blinding
"hotspot" on the glass, which the engineers tried to eliminate
for years. No matter how much genius they applied to finally
diffusing it away, that hot spot always glared back at them from
the center of the bulb.

Every seasoned engineer knew you simply couldn't get
rid of it. The joke was pulled on every new engineer coming into
the department. Fresh from college, each newbie was assigned
the task of creating what couldn't be created: a coating that would
smear the brightness across the surface of the bulb, eliminating
the hotspot.

The veterans snickered, waiting for their fresh-faced
victim to return, surrender in hand and worried about failing his
first assignment. It was an engineer's version of "snipe hunting."

One day, however, a would-be victim walked out with
what we now know as the "Soft White" light bulb. He handed over
to his peers exactly what they were certain couldn't be created.

Moral of the story? No one told the rookie that the coating
couldn't be created, so he created it.

The echoes that scrape the inside of my mind this evening
like a pumpkin being prepared for a Halloween carving are the
reminders of all I wanted my life to be. Reminders of things I
intended to stand for, accomplish, and produce before a long line
of "elders" told me they couldn't be done.

Sometimes I wonder if most peer groups exist in some
small way to inform the idealistic ones that their dreams are dead
on arrival. How many things did you dream of doing, being, that

someone more experienced in life quashed by informing you it couldn't be done?

What's worse, I've discovered the person kicking the stilts out from under my own dreams is me; my own voice has become the one telling me what I've dreamt is impossible to realize.

Sometimes, on quiet nights when I am brave enough to listen, the echoes of who I expected to be insist otherwise.

A Good Day Off

[Originally Published by Leadership Journal]
This season was the busiest in recent memory. Our church just began building an addition to our facility. Though excited about breaking ground, I sensed the construction was adding bricks to a growing wall between my family and me.

My wife, Cheryl, and I lamented how detached our family had become. The kids filled their days in the isolated world of television. And the growing numbers of people at church were tyrannizing my calendar. A new youth pastor, youth camps, additions to buildings, new member classes, Bible studies, discipleship, visits … aaaahh!

I decided we needed to get away—to rescue our ministry from burnout and to retrieve our marriage from strain. We took our Sunday evening through Monday evening "day off" and journeyed to Willow Creek—the one in Beaverhead National Forest, not the one in Illinois. A day and a half to find our sense of family again. No phones, no computers, no people, and no TV.

The first indication of the Lord's blessing on our trip was our cell phone's "no service" message flashing at us. The drive through a narrow canyon back to Hollow Top Mountain not only separated us from 21st century communications, it took us to South Willow Creek, where the water is so clear you can read the date off a dime five feet deep.

We set up a tent for Cheryl and me, and one for our daughters, Madison and Baylee, and our son, Hayden, whom we affectionately call "Spartacus." With tents pitched, we started a fire that would keep us company into the wee hours of the morning.

After the last s'more was consumed (defined as the one that makes you sick), it was bedtime.

We wedged the kids into sleeping bags, prayed with them, left them a flashlight, and assured them that bears slept at night (and that dad often sleeps with his 12 gauge, just for kicks). They giggled for 20 minutes and fell asleep, which gave Cheryl and me time to settle back in lawn chairs and warm ourselves by the fire.

It was an intimate fire, painting itself in shifting subtleties of blues. Which is nice for looking at stars. When you are 50 miles from town and several thousand feet high, it becomes more of a challenge to find sky than stars. It looked like God had spilled a pouch of diamonds on the floor of heaven, and we sat bedazzled by the sparkle on the ceiling of Earth. It is easy to feel small sitting beneath the theater of the heavens.

It's also easy to blather on about everything you haven't talked to your wife about for months, or years. And blather we did—for hours. Each new log seemed to give us a new topic, and the creek provided background music.

Our conversations started small, carved through perspectives, poured into larger topics, got obscured in unrelated issues, and eventually wound back to the starting point. It was effortless, unlike conversations at home, where the words have to be pried from our mouths like bad teeth. Here, they flowed like the melted snow behind us.

The next morning, we took the children to seek the native Cutthroat trout.

The thrill of catching the trout wasn't coaxing them from beneath the turbulent pocketwater or how readily they took a #12 PartridgeWinkle. The thrill of catching these fish was watching my kids reel them in; I don't know that I've ever seen such honest expressions of wonder and excitement on their faces as when they took the rod from my hand and realized there was something on the other end. It's better than Disneyland.

Seven-year-old Madison lunged toward me from the bank to be the first one to reel in a fish. She slipped on a rock and struggled to catch her breath in the frigid water. But when she hoisted the Cut from the water, she gave it a kiss. Hayden stared at the little trout he caught and giggled like he had met a new friend.

Five-year-old Baylee and I shared a serendipitous moment that passed as quickly as it came. Our first six casts together each yielded a fish. I hooked them and she played them like a master, holding her rod tip high and reeling slowly. She stood like a mini-Hemingway commanding a mini-whale. She has potential.

But potential won't get you the 12-inch Cutthroat I stuck on the last cast. Whenever a trout rolls under the surface after being hooked instead of running, you take a Lamaze-style cleansing breath, sanctify yourself, and prepare for the challenge. This one rolled.

The fish leapt, trying to fly away. It turned downstream, hoping to use the power and speed of the current to break away. It raced upstream, attempting to find enough slack to shake loose from the #12. I felt the shock, heard the anger, battled the determination, sensed the panic, and responded to the fish's resignation in succession.

What a fish! He rested in the palm of my hand, his spotted tail slapping my forearm, his orange fins trying to swim through the air. I showed him to Baylee. She gave him a kiss. I gave him a kiss too, and we let him go.

Twelve inches doesn't seem like much. But on a high mountain stream the width of a few sidewalks, underneath a canopy of pines, a 12-inch fish is a Titan. The disciples can keep the 153 fish caught on the Sea of Galilee; give me one 12-inch Cutthroat at 6,500 feet.

We walked back to camp, weaving our way through the ancient growth of pine trees and soft carpet of decaying pine needles. Baylee said with her typical enthusiasm, *"We're great fisherman, aren't we, Dad?"*

"We sure are, Bayls," I said.

"We really knocked 'em dead, didn't we, Dad?"

"We sure did, Bayls."

"I don't want to go home," she said.

Those were the sweetest words I think I've ever heard. I would never have imagined the treasure stored in a simple day off. Not that I haven't taken one before, but I haven't used one like that in a long time. I realized once again the pleasure of my family and found refreshment for my future.

Jesus made a habit of getting away from the multitudes. I think He knew the blessings found in time away. Sometimes the best way to enjoy our families is to get away with them.

It doesn't take a lot of money; it doesn't require an amusement park. All it takes is a simple day off.

An Incomplete Education

Anyone who's watched kids go off to college probably recognizes the sinking feeling that accompanies the bleak recognition of all the things you overlooked when teaching them about life. Mine came on a short, inconsequential walk down our street before driving Mad to Chicago for college.

I don't even remember how the subject came up on our stroll, but somehow we got around to talking about home mortgages. Mad stopped in the street, looked at me and her mom with waves of shock, and said, *"You mean people haven't paid for these houses?"*

No. They have not.

That was my first tip that there were freight train-sized gaps in the education I had given my oldest child.

That education started with the most important lesson I believed needed to be taught. When Mad was carrying-size and in my arms most everywhere we went, I'd occasionally ask her, *"Who loves you?"*

"Mommy!" she'd begin.

"Who else?"

"Gramma! Grampa!"

I could tell she was trying to think of people to prolong the fun; Mad loved any chance to be loud and wouldn't let the opportunity end so quickly. She was also correct.

"Yes, they do ... Who else loves you?"

"Daddy!" she yelled louder, throwing herself back and raising her arms up like she just scored a touchdown.

What dad doesn't love to hear those words? The payoff in her exuberance wasn't that I loved her, nor that she acknowledged I loved her; it was that she seemed so happy I did.

And I did and do, but I always asked one more time, *"Who else?"*

"God!" she belted out again, seizing her bonus yell with abandon.

"Yes! He does!" I bounced her up and down and added, *"Just a liiiittle bit more than I do."*

The last part was hard to say but easy to believe. I can't conceive of anyone loving my kids more than I, but I also know it's true. The first thing I wanted imprinted on her little life was that God loves her more than anyone. Even me.

I've discovered, however, that she wasn't the only one learning something in those questions.

On a Wednesday night last April, Cheryl got a text saying Mad was in the hospital in New York State. She had stomach problems and was throwing up a lot. "Sinking feeling" doesn't quite touch the wobbly legs I tried to steady when I heard it.

I hate the feeling of helplessness when it comes to my kids. I felt it when Mad was savagely attacked by a dog in 1996 and again when Baylee was almost four and appeared to be dead after suffering what turned out to be a harmless seizure.

I also felt it with Hayden when he was two; stomach pain kept him crying all day. After our doctor couldn't pinpoint the problem, he feared it was an appendicitis. He told me he wanted to call in a surgeon to "open him up and look around," like my boy was an Oldsmobile with a knock in the engine.

I consented. What good are doctors if you can't trust them? However, when the surgeon arrived, he asked Spartacus to bend over and touch his toes and do a few other contortions which apparently confirmed this wasn't an appendicitis.

As the surgeon was telling me the procedure would have to be more exploratory in nature, Hayden farted so loudly it registered on the Richter Scale as far away as Albuquerque and sent local Doomsday Preppers grabbing for their "go-bags" thinking Yellowstone was about to blow.

We all looked at him on the bed; he was just smiling like he had hit a home run in the bottom of the ninth.

Anyway ...

So Mad recovered. Everything was and is alright; it was gastroenteritis, and a change in diet was all the prescription she required. She has insurance through her school, and she went on with her college's singing tour.

In each event where my kids have come into close orbit with tragedy, what I held onto was the little lesson I first taught Madison while hoisting her in my arms: God loves them more than I do.

Her incomplete education seemed to rear its ugly head every semester's end when her money fell short of her college bill. Mad was fined for making late payments, which were given past due even when she had the money to make them.

I explained to her that, not only do Bible Colleges want their money just like any other college, they don't care if you have it in the bank. They care if you give it to them. When it's due.

It's not all her fault; she spent the first semester babysitting for a loony, wealthy woman who preferred to pay in used clothing. When we encouraged her to find other work, Mad said the kids were neglected and she hated to quit because of them. Consequently, she went nearly a semester without working ... or, rather, without being paid for working.

Second semester, she snagged a job at Victoria's Secret on the Miracle Mile in Chicago; her success there was greater than any dad's comfort level. Nevertheless, Mad was often working until 2 a.m., which is not good on grades, and she remained short on tuition at the end of the school year.

So, she planned on a two-job summer, arranging both a babysitting job and receiving assurances she could work at the Victoria's Secret in Bozeman. Not only would this give her extra money for next year's tuition, but it would hold her job in Chicago by keeping her in their system.

After a month home, Victoria's Secret hadn't scheduled her. Madison assumed each week that the next week's schedule would have her on it; it didn't. They simply never had her down to work and, worse, they never told her. Now she was out of their system and wasn't guaranteed a job at the store in Chicago.

Finally, she told us she wanted to take an interim semester off from school. The college she attends is selective and space is limited, so students are allowed only one semester off without penalty in order to earn money and return the following semester.

As long as it's approved.

Mad told us worrying about money the previous school year had eaten at her and probably contributed to her stomach problems. Her plan was to get enough funding before going back so she wouldn't be continually behind, continually worried about bills and continually working.

I'm always leery about "time off"; it usually leads to "life off." When we talked, I told her the essence of my concern, which was that the world is littered with people who have 30 college credits and a job at JiffyLube because they took a semester off and never returned. I just couldn't see her working at JiffyLube.

We discussed the rules for staying and what I expected. I pressed her on the decision because I wanted her to be sure; she promised to think on it more.

Then, she got a bill from the hospital in New York. The insurance hadn't paid for it all, and she owed them $1,000. She was crying, overwhelmed by the financial facts of life. It was also the last straw.

With the extra bill, Mad couldn't go back and made plans to stay with us until January. She applied for her Interim Semester, began to look for more work and took an ill-advised 3 a.m.–5:30 a.m. gig delivering newspapers; at least the kid's not afraid of work.

Cheryl and I settled into the secretly comfortable notion of having her home for the next four months. In spite of our earlier misgivings, we knew how hard the last year had been on her, and seeing the next shaping up to be worse, we approved.

Her college didn't.

Four weeks until she had to return or possibly never go back, Mad got the official reply. No, she wasn't eligible for this Interim Semester, and she must to return in August or lose her place.

Our daughter was thousands short of the tuition needed and had no time to get it. With the money monster staring her in the face, she started crying. A lot. And then some more.

She was distraught and I was frustrated. Grappling again with that helpless feeling only my kids can generate, I wondered how I could live so long and not be able to help my daughter get back to college.

Then ...

A young woman in our church told Mad she wanted to send her $100 a month while she was in school.

A pastor in whose church Mad had done some singing found out she was short on her medical bill and called her saying he and his church wanted to give her $500 toward covering it.

One of our deacons offered for our church to pay for her books.

My mom promised to send her $200/month while she was in school.

Our church Trustees (without my saying a word) have asked to meet with her for the purpose of helping her in a significant way.

As of today, it turns out she may not have much of a bill at all when she arrives back on campus in 16 days.

As these reports rolled in, I took her aside and told her she was seeing this windfall because she was a vital part of a church. She had been raised in this congregation. She had served and ministered to people in our community. Her brother and sister were pleasant fixtures in a church her parents had faithfully served for years.

Moreover, I urged her to remember how she had given faithfully to others when they were in need. She had shown consistent love for the community of believers in her church.

Now, they were loving her back. More precisely, God was loving her through them.

Madison, like everyone, certainly has some gaps in life education, but the lesson she really needed was that love usually finds its way back to those who give it and that God really does know the end from the beginning.

I discovered, however, we were both taking a remedial course in essential life lessons. In my frustration over not being able to provide for the daughter I loved so much, I was relearning the earliest lesson I taught her in my arms when she was a baby.

God showed me that the person who needs to trust in His surpassing love for my daughter is oftentimes her dad.

"Who loves you, Madison?"

"Daddy!"

"Yes, he does. Who loves you, Madison?"

"God!"

"Yes! Just a liiiittle more than I do."

And I'd have it no other way.

Ordinary

Walked in the door and wandered through the house.

We had just arrived home from the former Gallatin Field. It's now called "Bozeman-Yellowstone International Airport," an apparent concession to the privileged and celebrities who frequent Big Sky, Montana, like royalty slumming among the local serfs. It must have seemed altogether too gauche to tell everyone back home that they were flying to lowly "Gallatin Field," as if they were jetting into some Quonset with a lone wind sock and a guy named "Mitch" who mowed the grass on the runway.

So the name changed to reflect a more sophisticated clientele. At least, that's my explanation for the change since "Bozeman-Yellowstone International Airport" is neither in Bozeman nor near Yellowstone and has no commercial international flights. But it is a very nice airport and its cleanliness and simplicity and beauty cushion the blow for parents sending their daughter back to college.

It was a more or less quiet ride home and, after a quarter-hour trying to find something to do that would make us appear unaffected by the silence of Mad's now-summer room spilling out into the rest of the house, Cheryl and I decided to lie down together. I suppose it would have been mildly scandalous on a routine afternoon, but lying on our bed would accomplish

the same amount of nothing had we sat behind a desk staring
at a screen, mindlessly opened cabinet doors, or walked down
hallways pointlessly trying to adjust to the invasion of emptiness
in our home.

We lay there. Cheryl's head was resting on my shoulder,
and we talked about things. And life. We sighed some, confessed
sadness we thought had been disguised, and laughed enough to
keep us safely removed from depression.

It all came down to this: here we were—Steve and
Cheryl—and our oldest was flying off to her second year in
college, our middle daughter was days away from her last year of
high school, and Spartacus, my youngest, would begin high school
in a week.

We marveled at us for awhile and spoke gently to one
another as we surveyed the ripples of life flattening out behind us.

"We all turn out pretty ordinary." The sentence came from
nowhere, and it was half said before I realized it was out loud.

"What?" Cheryl whispered.

I was looking at a picture on the wall next to my side of
the bed that had been suspended there since we moved in over ten
years ago. It's small and there is a spot on the glass wiped clear of
dust to better show our kids' faces in the photo. I wiped that spot
months ago and it was now well into getting a fresh coat of dusty
blur.

Only God knows how many times I had looked over at
it—before bed, in the mornings stretching away the back and
shoulder aches, sitting in the chair reading, or watching TV. But
there they are: frozen in time.

They are the children I once knew, and, unlike today, their
height is according to birth order in the frame. Their smiles pierce
the dust and reflect the exuberance of kids on holiday; they are
dressed for Easter in the old building our church occupied.

Madison and Baylee are sporting corsages I bought
them for the morning, and Spart is wearing clothes that have no

Nebraska Cornhusker "N" on them anywhere—surprising, even on Easter. They are there together, close knit and beautiful. I imagine them anxious to get home and sift through Easter baskets with Grandma.

"*Ordinary,*" I said again. "*We all turn out pretty ordinary.*"

"*What do you mean?*"

"*I just remember when I was the age they are now; when I was twenty, I felt pretty extraordinary. I walked past people in the painfully ordinary neighborhoods doing painfully ordinary chores and knee-deep in painfully ordinary routines, and I just knew my life held more than the ordinary.*"

She understood what I meant; we knew it when we were dating and in the initial years of marriage. I don't know if we would have phrased it as such, but we had never intended to be ordinary. God's purpose was magnificent; the ministry needed our fresh faces and our collective idealism would carry us up and over the riptide of ordinary that imprisoned the masses.

"*And here we are,*" I continued. "*Middle-aged and the kids we never dreamed we'd have are about to leave for lives of their own ... No one ever tells you that when you have children you surrender the next twenty years of life making sure they are fed, sheltered, and capable of becoming better people than you were and all God wants them to be.*

With the resigned voice of remembrance, my thoughts continued, "*Twenty years ... Twenty years of the most ordinary stuff life ever served up: oil changes, parent meetings, crusty noses, Sunday School, hand-me-downs, yard work, Christmas trees, Tickle Monsters, owies, Back-to-School, and all the other mundanities I never realized I was enjoying while pressing through them so I could focus on being extraordinary.*"

"*Yeah,*" Cheryl agreed. "*Nothing wrong with ordinary.*"

No. There isn't.

There are three souls on this planet who never needed me to be extraordinary. They never needed me to pastor thousands, write books, be known by scores of people, or pursue my extraordinariness.

They needed me to count their breaths as they lay wheezing with a respiratory infection, making sure they were doing alright. They needed me to be home at night and slip into their rooms and stare at them sleeping and silently pray for them.

They needed me to sneak out with them in the middle of the night to get some pop for no reason at all and to carry them like a "sack o' taters" to bed. They needed me to worry about gas mileage and to work out the fights I had with their mom and ask to see their report cards and take family pictures and give them hugs for no reason and a myriad other daily routines I swore would never mark my life.

They needed me to be ordinary.

As I lay there next to my wife, I understood for the first time the beauty of it—of ordinary.

"Guess not."

I could feel Cheryl's eyelids blink against my shoulder, and I wondered what she was thinking. Outside, we heard the familiar sound of straining engines as a plane burst into the sky from Bozeman-Yellowstone International Airport.

"There she goes," I eked out.

I felt Cheryl smile as a corner of her mouth moved against my chest. And we stayed there just a few minutes longer, listening to the engines in the sky fade into the east and squeezing each other a little tighter as a small reward for being so ordinary for so long.

CHAPTER 7
....

REDEMPTION & TAPESTRY

Cold and Lonely

My grandpa was a depot agent. Probably a lot of people don't know what a "depot agent" ever was; they couldn't know what it *is*, because my grandpa was one of the last to ever hold the title.

He was a lifer with the Chicago, Burlington and Quincy Railroad, working the depots along its mainline that sliced through southeastern Nebraska before it took a hard right at Lincoln and barreled west for Denver. When "The Q" merged with three other railroads on my birthday in 1970, my grandpa became a holdover employee that the newly created Burlington Northern Railroad reluctantly shuffled among its dilapidated depots until they could pull the plug on the local agencies altogether.

Until the mid-twentieth century, railroad depots were staples in every granger town that dotted the landscape throughout the gut of America. On the Burlington, the agents manning a station in those communities usually lived with their families in the second-floor living quarters of the depots they worked during the day—a kind of railroad "parsonage."

My grandparents raised a couple kids along the tracks, including my dad. According to him, there were significant challenges associated with living next to the mainline of a Class 1 railroad.

Getting a good night's sleep was nearly impossible with the California Zephyr streaking passengers to the coast and routine freight trains racing the sunrise to Chicago. Also, with his front yard being ten feet of brick platform that ended at the tracks, my dad gave up on dog ownership at an early age.

Memories of my grandpa begin here, in the lower portion of the depot in Gretna, Nebraska. Every summer of my childhood, I was a fixture there, accompanying my grandpa as he bided his time in a job as antiquated as the steady Regulator clock on the wall.

From this depot, I drove my first—and last—train when my grandpa told me to yell up at the engineer to *"Show me the motor!"* Apparently that meant, *"Hey! Let this seven-year-old drive that billion-ton train,"* because that's exactly what he did, for about 100 yards.

Placed next to the tired, coal-oil stove in the center of the dusty room were stuffed leather chairs that sat low to the ground and looked like they had been delivered by the Pony Express. The sharp, deep creases in the seats had been slathered in with grime from decades of section crews' butts sinking into them while warming next to the stove on icy winter days.

Whether from my grandpa or one of the weathered section men who would drop by, I sat in those old gnarled chairs and listened to colorful stories while eating my cheese sandwich and drinking heavily creamed coffee with enough sugar that it pooled on the bottom of the cup. I heard tales of runaway trains, cruel railroad "bulls," and ordinary men who made sure America kept humming; unknown to me, these recollections were the oral canon of a time dying before my eyes.

I wish I could remember them all. These times were my childhood vocation. They don't quite reach the level of "magical," but it was close enough for me.

My grandpa's was one of the first jobs that was a casualty of emerging technology and the so-called convenience of airlines. As dirt roads turned to superhighways and passenger jets littered the sky, fewer and fewer people traveled by train, and, facing the twilight of their careers, depot agents traded in their keys to the freight house for those of utilitarian Chevrolet vans.

By the mid-sixties, the ancient, inefficient depots built at the turn-of-the-century were abandoned by the railroad in favor of "Mobile Agencies." A complete inversion of standard railroad practice, the mobile agents travelled by cargo van to the customers and used two-way radios, file cabinets, and typewriters tucked away in the cargo space to write orders that had previously come to *them* for a century.

Fortunately for my grandpa, retirement was a merciful few years away. He left the railroad just as depots, depot agents, and another cohesive bond within small towns were dismantled by an industry searching for a profit by eliminating overhead.

"Retirement," however, was a word I didn't understand at eight years old. I remember dimly the night my parents told me my grandpa was no longer working for the railroad and I wouldn't be going back to the depot again. I sobbed. They might as well have told me he died.

I don't think I've ever gotten over it.

This is all a long introduction to a picture that accompanied me through childhood. It's one of those mementos that burns itself into your mind and is as sharp on the day you crest middle-age as it was when your bedtime was before the late news.

It's a small, loosely framed picture of my grandpa cut from a newspaper article in The Omaha World Herald. It was first propped up in his house and then my room after he retired. I guess it was something he thought would soften the blow a little.

The picture was yellowed when I inherited it, and only recently have I seen the entire article that image of him adorned; a quick search of the World Herald archives found it in 0.16

seconds. Ironic that "Technology" helped eliminate my grandpa's job, then enables me to remember it.

The article was written in 1967, the year after I was born, and was a harbinger of the demise of such depots as I described. The picture contains all the elements I loved about my mostly summer afternoons spent as an unpaid Agent's Sidekick along the CB&Q.

The desk beneath the bay window was warmly cluttered with all the office supplies of mid-century, and the unique railroad phone hung suspended over them. This phone was maybe the first "mobile" one of its kind. It was attached to an expandable/ retractable arm and the earpiece was designed to be worn over the head by a metal arch, much like what a pilot in WWII would have worn while dropping bombs on jungle islands.

The individual panes of the bay window, even in the photograph, seemed to leak cold February air. Beyond them was my grandpa, outside, wearing his ubiquitous hat and clutching train orders. He appears to be walking across the red-brick platform; a boxcar still sporting the livery of the merged Northern Pacific Railroad is in the background.

Everything in that photo was old and outdated, even forty-seven years ago. Yet, it was perfect, capturing everything I loved about the wonder of the days I'll never forget with my grandpa. I gazed at it countless times in my bedroom as a kid when I was bored or banished there as punishment or afraid of the dark.

It comforted me. In an inexplicable way, it warmed me.

There was a little more to the picture that I never paid much attention to, something that seemed incidental to the image when I was a boy. It was the caption on the bottom of the photograph which read: *"Agent L.E. Van Winkle at Ralston ... Sometimes a cold, lonely job."*

I was never able to reconcile that mournful caption with the memory of my grandpa's vocation. As you might have surmised, I thought his was the pinnacle of all occupations, that a job as depot agent couldn't be topped by any trade, calling, or vocation in the world.

"Cold, lonely? You can't be serious," I concluded as a kid, and rarely, if ever, gave the notion of "cold and lonely" a perceptible thought again.

I sent that picture to my dad many moons ago. I'm not sure why, but I probably just figured it was his dad and he'd like to have some token for his own memories; mine were vivid enough. I've not seen the picture again until my World Herald search the other day. The image was just how I had left it in my mind, but that incredulous caption caught my eye in a way it never had when I was a boy.

"Sometimes a cold, lonely job."

Thirty-five years have passed since I took notice of that caption, and in that time something has happened. Those words have become three-dimensional. And personal.

Every weekend, I'm in the midst of a crowd of people who listen to me preach and take notes and nod their heads. Usually, I talk with dozens of people each week about any number of things. Sometimes they're hovering over my shoulder, waiting to chat with me, invite me over, or compliment me. It's the epitome of warm and communal.

When the door closes behind the last one, however, the first nip of cold air seems to leak through the panes of the approaching week's tasks. It's when I feel the first pings of "cold and lonely" in a vocation most would perceive as neither.

Sure, there are moments I'm surrounded by people and hours I spend with friends; when most people see me, I'm flanked by people wearing smiles. But there's no community when people have to be confronted; indeed, I've found few things quite as lonely. There's no camaraderie when people lay confidential burdens on my lap; these must be wrestled alone.

When the cold pressure of offerings and attendance grate on my ego, no one is standing in line to tell me what a "blessing" it is to hear my sermons. And after those who have invited me over for coffee or dinner leave the building, I'm still faced with the icy task of finding and coddling people waiting for a chance to say how the church is not meeting their needs and how disappointing I am.

When all the people go their way to live their life and church is left behind until the next Sunday, I'm still here. A lone parson overseeing what sometimes seems like an antiquated concept, facing tasks and people and routine and responsibility that can sometimes be described as ... cold and lonely.

I gazed at the image of my grandpa. It wasn't on the dresser of my bedroom anymore; it was on the screen of my laptop in a coffee shop. If the picture were altered, I thought—if the desk had commentaries and calendars and bulletins, if the bulky phone and headset was an iPhone, if the man outside the window was flanked by mountains and clutching a Bible—I wondered if the caption would read:

"Pastor S.R. Van Winkle at Bozeman ... Sometimes a cold, lonely job."

For all its joys and satisfactions, my job can seem isolated and alone. Most people wouldn't think of it as such, much like an eight-year-old couldn't conceive of his depot agent grandpa ever feeling cold and lonely alongside the busy mainline. I wonder now how funny my delight in his job must have seemed when cold and lonely were his daily companions.

I'm certain I would have spent my life in depots had they not died out before I had the chance to carry on my grandpa's legacy. Yet, while the ministry I have served for two decades in no way resembles the routine of a depot agent, at least I am able to identify with my grandpa in one way: while the railroad never became a Van Winkle tradition ...

Cold and Lonely runs in the family.

You Can Keep My Heart

For her eighteenth birthday, my daughter Baylee asked for something unique. Spurning the cars, cash, and electronic trinkets of all sorts, she asked me to write my life story for her.

I've received no end of compliments for having such a thoughtful daughter; it has evoked a variety of responses from disbelief to envy. What's really strange is that, while I did find it something of a curious request, it wasn't really a shock. That's Baylee. She's not normal in all the best ways.

Instead of causing me to reflect on my life, her preferred gift made me remember something about her. About a year after I was called to be pastor of Fellowship Baptist Church, the normal routine of that vocation ushered me into one of my favorite moments in life.

Since God was a boy, Independent Baptists have maintained a pretty consistent schedule of church services. In 1995, we hadn't veered much from the template laid out by our forefathers.

We met for a couple hours on Sunday morning and then had a scaled-down version of the same service that evening at 6pm. We also gathered on Wednesdays for what was originally known as a "Prayer Meeting," but prayer had long before been displaced by a lengthier mid-week Bible Study.

The year 1995 also found me and Cheryl following the standard template for families. After a little more than five years of marriage and one child already starting to go mobile, we were waiting on the second of our statistically predictable 2.5 kids.

We were old hands at kids by now, having already raised our first to the age of eighteen months with no casualties. We knew what to expect when we were expecting and had discovered that the principles of Lamaze were a source of unending annoyance once an actual child was being delivered. (I think

Cheryl's stuffed bear "focus object" had to be surgically extracted from the delivery room wall after she swatted it out of my hand during Madison's birth.)

So, we were set; we were on cruise control; we were veterans.

We were also parents who didn't want to know the gender of our kids before they were born. It probably sounds a little silly, but by not peeking through that veil, it seemed we were letting our kids surprise us with something personal about them instead of trying to divine it with technology for our curiosity or convenience.

It was as if they entered the world and told us, *"Hi! I'm a GIRL! ... Betcha didn't know that! ... What's my name? ... WAAAAHHHHH"*

Or something like that.

I've always grimaced on the inside when asking someone if they want a boy or a girl, and they respond, *"I just want a healthy baby."* No kidding. I guess I just assume everyone wants a healthy baby; perhaps I should rephrase the question to, *"Would you prefer a healthy boy or a healthy girl?"*

Madison took care of the healthy girl part; now I wanted a healthy boy.

By November, Cheryl's pregnancy had reached almost unbearable status. She was also sick. Constantly. She either had a cold or some unearthly stomach bug relentlessly compounding the usual discomfort of being pregnant.

When her misery peaked late one evening, this Independent Baptist almost called a priest.

Cheryl came out of the bedroom that night looking like she would have embraced death as an old friend if it would deliver her from the inhuman pain she endured. She sat down on the couch after giving up trying to sleep through some nausea. We started talking about nothing important when—in the middle of a sentence—vomit exploded from her mouth.

I mean, no warning, no heaving, no dry runs ... She was in the middle of a bland sentence when a volcano of ugliness erupted from her mouth where happy words once lived. Without moving or even trying to run to the bathroom, she leaned over and let the rest just flow onto the carpet for what seemed like an hour.

I had never seen anything like it; I was stunned. And terrified. I never admired Cheryl more than I did that night. Had it been me, I would have crawled into a corner and prayed for an asteroid the size of Greenland to strike the earth before this Devil-Child she carried was unleashed on mankind to initiate the apocalypse.

Cheryl just soldiered on, like moms do. From my perspective, however, the difference in pregnancies between Madison and Baylee is the difference between "She's Having a Baby," starring Kevin Bacon, and "Rosemary's Baby," starring Satan.

November was also the frayed end of our pregnancy nerves, Cheryl more than me, of course. Relief of any sort eluded her, and she arrived at the familiar point where people knew better than to ask, *"Haven't had that baby yet?"* or *"I'll bet you're ready for that baby to be born."*

Visions of Robert Stack punching his way through an airport come to mind.

The last Wednesday of November in 1995 was on the 29th. Cheryl arrived at church with Madison and took her usual seat. Everyone met in the auditorium for prayer requests, announcements, and maybe to sing a hymn. Afterward, we moved to a multi-purpose room where people sat at tables while I led a Bible study.

Nothing unusual about this Wednesday; we finished the preliminaries in the auditorium and shuffled back to the tables. While people found seats, I opened my notebook, adjusted the overhead projector, and was ready to begin about the time everyone was settled.

Then I heard it. My ears caught the loud whisper of *"Pssst!... Pssst! ... Pastor Steve ... "*

I looked over my left shoulder to see a dear, faithful lady in our church standing in the hallway out of sight of those at the tables. She was semi-crouched, like she was trying to maintain a low profile in the dim corridor; she was waving at me to come to her.

I walked over, feeling my brow raise, silently inviting her to tell me what was so important to interrupt our Bible study.

"Cheryl's water just broke."

[Blink, blink] I felt my brow scrunch, silently indicating I must not have heard correctly (I do a lot of talking with my eyebrows). *"What?"*

"Cheryl's water broke ... It's time."

"Ummm ... When?"

"Now. She needs to go now."

"To the hospital?"

"Yes."

I don't remember clearly, but I think she may have grown a little amused at this point. Honestly, I lost all ability to think in complete sentences.

I walked back out into the room stuffed with people who had now determined I was gone long enough for it to be unusual. For the first and last time, I noticed people staring at me when I was in front of them.

"Uhh ... Hmmm ... Well, Jeanne just told me Cheryl's water broke ... So ... uhhh ..."

This is your brain ... This is your brain having just been told your wife's water broke in the church auditorium while about 70 people are waiting for the study to begin and you have no idea what to do about the service or your 18 month old who will need a way home while you're at the hospital: *Scrambled.*

"So ... I guess ..." I looked back over at Jeanne who I think had meandered into the room by now. I glanced back at the people, and they were all smiling.

"Uhh ... well ... right ... I guess ..."

212

I was just about to suggest that I could finish the service because, after all, being a veteran of kids, I know that babies don't come immediately after water breaks. In its scrambled state, brains often suggest immensely stupid things, but just before I uttered it, a man spoke up.

"You just need to get out of here." Tony was another dear friend whose enjoyment of and comfort in being goofy belied both his spiritual depth and concern for others.

"We'll take care of everything," he continued. Someone else said they would take Mad home with them.

I think I started to refuse. I know it pales in comparison, but of all the things in my life I can easily brush aside, I have always had a keen sense of privilege and responsibility when it comes to God's house. It just didn't feel right to walk out of church.

A collective *"Get out of here!"* shocked me back into coherence, so I grabbed Cheryl and left. We made a stop at the apartment and drove to Bozeman Deaconess Hospital, arriving around 8:00 p.m.

"Precious" is not a word I find much use for, but looking back, if ever there have been truly precious moments in my life, at least a few of them have taken place in the halls of Bozeman Deaconess in the hours preceding the birth of our kids. Those memories are treasures.

The nurses always encouraged us to walk around to help kickstart the birth; we always did. Cheryl had a jug of Pitocin dripping into her veins, and the business-casual hallways of Bozeman Deaconess were permeated with a whiff of ammonia leaking through the medical offices.

We strolled like it was spring in Paris, talking about life and marriage and the kid we had and the family we were building. We talked about our love, our hopes, our dreams, and our future.

We talked about you, Baylee.

There's nothing like an unflattering hospital gown, a nervous dad, and the anticipation of a miracle to get a husband and wife talking. And we did. We spent those hours marveling at our blessings and confessing our fears. We were too young and too poor to have kids, but we were too excited to care.

I don't know that I have any fonder memories in my life than I do of those walks.

Baylee, I fell asleep in a chair next to your mom's bed. At some point after midnight, when the date flopped to the 30th, doctors and nurses assembled.

We dispensed with the focus objects, and your mom set about the labor of childbirth. You were born sharing the same birthday as your "Uncle" who's not related to me ... I'll just call him Uncle "John L. Smith."

"One more good push!" With that, Dr. Benda's arms swung out and away from your mom and ... there you were.

We've told you this, but you had a pointy head and crazy hair standing straight up on top of it. Dr. Benda and the nurses gave a relieved sounding cheer, and you looked at us and said ...

"Hi! I'm a GIRL! ... Betcha didn't know that! ... What's my name?"

Your mom answered, *"You're Baylee."*

They walked you over to her and laid you on her chest. When Madison was born, your mom had some complications, and she didn't get to enjoy the moment she shared with you.

I remember her looking down and flashing a mom's smile. I've never smiled at you like she did; I never will. It's a smile the Lord only gives to moms.

But I did hear you talk to me as she bathed you in that smile; it was in a voice only dads can hear. You looked at me and said...

"Hi dad. I'm here to steal your heart; I'll never give it back to you, either. Don't worry, you'll still love me with a depth no one's invented a word for yet, and, in exchange, I promise to rescue

you from all sorts of despair with magical hugs. I promise you'll be proud of me.

"I know you wanted a boy, but, trust me, I'm better. Oh, one last thing, dad, I may give you reason to worry at times, but you'll never be able to resist telling me you love me and hugging me every chance you get. Feel free to stop by my cradle and my bed when I'm sleeping and wonder and pray."

It's amazing, Baylee. Everything you told me on the day you were born is exactly what has happened.

I've told the beginning of this story, pal; you'll write the end. But I know this and I hope you always remember these things: Love brought you into our family, and your birth began in the household of faith and you share a birthday with a person whose friendship I've never questioned.

As you continue to write the chapters of your journey, never forget those are the three essentials of life. When you find love, as you continue in the faith and discover lifelong, faithful friends ... you've found everything.

And you can keep my heart, buddy. Always.

One of Them

Since I was 12 or 13, I knew in rough sketch the guy I wanted to be. I wanted to be the missing guy; I wanted to be the discontented guy; I wanted to be the exile.

Growing up, I couldn't imagine anything more wasteful than to squander my life where I was raised: Lincoln, Nebraska. Lincoln was hot; it was humid; it was boring; it was nondescript; it was bland; it was an oasis for underachievers. It was Lincoln. It was Nebraska.

What I wanted was mountains, rivers, life-threatening weather. I wanted to master things no one else had heard of; I wanted mystique. Mostly, I wanted to succeed at something no other friend was brave enough to attempt: leaving.

I always saw myself as the guy who "returned"—the one no one can find for the reunion and the one who rides the storm home for Christmas. I guess it was an adolescent snobbery of sorts. I was too good for the "good life," and I wanted to let Nebraska and the people there know how much I didn't need them or their predictable futures.

I succeeded on some counts, I guess. I am the one who "returns." I am the one who had to be tracked down for the reunion. I am the one who people "hear" has come to town.

I am the exile. Which is goody for me, I suppose.

Yet, something's changed. The romance encased in slugging on through storms to spend holidays at home has faded; not only is it a nuisance, I don't have a "home" anymore, at least not one I can go back to. There are also times when I miss not being known. Certainly people know me, but it's different.

One thing I couldn't have known when planning my exile is that life moves forward relentlessly. Like me, the people I left behind moved on with living, and on the occasions I returned to Lincoln, I never called any of my friends from high school.

If I saw a few close ones, I called it good.

Friendships aren't convenient a thousand miles away, and when there is nothing to keep them current, the urgent and the nearby soon monopolize all our attention. I was neither urgent nor nearby, and neither were they, so the bonds that tied us together eventually dissolved from neglect.

Simply moving away wasn't all that deleted relationships from my youth. I abandoned others in the name of Christ. Zealousness often accompanies conversion, and with mine I felt compelled to insistently inform my few remaining friends that they were on a greased slide heading for hell.

Honestly, those are the exact words I used. Really.

My motives were clean, but in an effort to draw childhood friends to the Best Friend I ever found—Jesus—I enthroned myself as the keymaster to eternity whom God had sent to enlighten their reprobate minds. Mostly, I confined my remarks to making sure they were aware God disapproved of their lifestyles.

Run into the arms of Jesus, I said, and they could be like me: upstanding, clean cut, right-thinking. They didn't appreciate that message much, and I didn't appreciate their lack of appreciation.

Eventually, what we all *did* appreciate was not talking to each other.

Thus, I achieved my goal: I was the exile. I lived in Montana, and in the name of Christ, I successfully separated myself from the influence of people I once called friends in order to maintain my own purity.

They rushed on with their lives, much like I did. And they wrestled with their own demons, much like I did. And they celebrated their milestones, much like I did. And they hugged their children and argued with their wives and studied for their careers and concerned themselves with their futures and enjoyed the little oases of relief from the thumbscrews of responsibility that tighten more every day, much like I did.

Everything continued as it had for 20 years. In the name of convenience and Christ, they lived their lives, and I lived in forgotten exile.

Until one of us died.

I've told you about my friend Jim dying. I guess this is the rest of the story.

In a lonely room on the campus of Boston Baptist College where I was preparing to teach a class on writing, I received a phone call. On the other end was my first best friend's ex-wife, Julie, who was also an old girlfriend of mine. She asked me to do Jim's eulogy.

I suppose we who leave with a chip on our shoulder secretly hope a call will find us one day asking us to come home and carry the moment. Speaking strictly in terms of what I hoped would eventually happen when I left Lincoln immediately after graduation, being given center stage at the most high profile, highly attended, post-high school event exceeded the wildest of wild expectations.

I never imagined someone, let alone my own friend, would have to die for that hope to be realized. It didn't feel like I thought it would; in fact, I felt sick.

I hadn't been a meaningful part of Jim's life for nearly twenty-five years; how could I do a eulogy after an absence that long? Julie assured me she had addressed that: I would speak about Jim's life through the high school years, and another friend, Mike, would handle the post-me decades. This would work, I thought.

Mike cancelled. He didn't think he could get through it. I suppose the unspoken assumption in his words was that, since I am a pastor, I *could* get through it. As the moment drew closer, I had grave doubts.

Whatever the reason, I was the last eulogist standing. This exile, the Baptist reverend, was given the microphone in one of Lincoln's largest Lutheran churches. Over five hundred were expected at the funeral, among whom were friends and family as well as faculty and students from my old high school where Jim had taught math for almost twenty years.

I felt sick. Again. I was also beginning to feel more and more like a schmuck.

Death is a leveling wind and seems to wipe away pretense and pomposity as mercilessly as an F5 tornado rips through a hapless mobile home. The pall of Jim's death made me feel very, very small. Not so much in comparison to it, but small as a human, as a person.

If it wasn't Jim Crew, I would have declined the invitation to speak. But I owed him this; truly, I owe him much more. Sadly, this was all there was left I could give.

The crowd was comprised of all those from whom I had been separated for the last two and a half decades. My erstwhile friends were now the support to Jim's family in a way I couldn't be; they had earned that right by staying and living and remaining in touch and being there.

I was the Exile.

And I was walking into twenty-five years of history as the final voice on the life of a man I had known mostly as a boy. That boy had graduated from the University of Nebraska and secured his dream job, married his high school sweetheart, and fathered four daughters now aged 7–15 whom he loved more than life itself.

I felt very conscious of my own pettiness and revisited every decision made on "principle" that led me away from these people who once were my friends. I would have been relieved to feel like a schmuck; as it was, I felt like an ass.

The night before the funeral we gathered together on Jim's driveway and did what all people do when someone dies and survivors don't want to cry: we reminisced. It was almost seamless; for a night on that driveway, there was no separation between any of us.

Stories that have been told over and over were told once more as a memorial to our friend; we immortalized him that evening in our laughter. I sat and laughed with the same guys who I once made sure knew exactly where they were spending eternity and whom I made aware of exactly what Jesus thought of their parties and their language and their disdain for the Bible.

They still drank their beer, they still cussed occasionally, and they still didn't seem to want me to preach to them. But, for one night, we were boys again, *friends* again.

I listened to their memories of Jim, and, after a time, I realized I knew these stories. I lived these stories. They weren't talking about Jim the college student or Jim the teacher or even Jim the dad. They were talking about Jim, my first best friend.

The world will continue, the Bible will be taught, some will be saved, and eternity will run its course, but this was a night to remember something I think I forgot, or maybe never learned. Namely, that the people we grow up with move us in a way no one else ever can, no matter how old we are.

I'm 41, and I remember these men when they were seven, thirteen, seventeen; that experience and relationship is somehow planted way down deep inside. I don't expect that we'll all be best friends, but I now know the years shared when we were kids tie us together in a way I never realized and still can't quite describe.

This epiphany stirred thoughts I didn't know I could have. It made me miss things I never thought I would. It made me long for things I thought were extraneous. It made me fear things I thought I was above.

After being introduced by a Lutheran minister in Birkenstocks, I stood the next morning before hundreds gathered for the memorial. I was on the verge of a breakdown and sensed pressure I have never, ever known. I hadn't eaten for days.

I looked down into the first two rows, saw Jim's family, and looked into the eyes of his daughters, whom I didn't know. To my left were the people from East High who had come in school colors; they looked like a pep club. An old girlfriend performed the solo, and in front of the casket were the friends I never lost, no matter how far away I tried to go or how spiritual I had become.

Everywhere I looked throughout the cavernous auditorium were memories in the faces of people I once knew.

I stood there, not as one who, in Jesus' name, had separated himself from these people a lifetime earlier, not as someone called in to save the moment, nor even as an exile. With tears constantly leaking from my eyes and a complete emotional breakdown imminent, I stood there as what I am, what I guess I always will be:

One of them.

Looking for Pheasants

Fathers' Day has always been a little cautionary for me. For the most part, it's a holiday I haven't remembered since I was twelve when my own dad walked out the door of our house on Father's Day, 1978.

It's never been intentional, mind you. It doesn't conceal brooding nor do I harbor latent resentment. It's just that, for the bulk of my life, I had as much reason to celebrate Father's Day as I did Secretary's Day.

Consequently, I've never noticed the approach of this holiday, even after I had kids of my own; indeed, the only reason I remember it at all is because parental holidays are overlooked in church only to the extreme peril of the pastor. Mother's and Father's Day are so highly regarded in congregations that I've sometimes wondered if people had kids simply to receive a rose or some other token after the special Sunday services in May and June.

And yet, I understand. I've saved almost every Father's Day card or tie or shaving kit or whatever that my kids have ever given me. I suppose they are my evidence that I have mattered to the people who will have the last say on the legacy of my life.

In a way I imagine only those who have had a parent leave can understand, I can't help but cast the joy I've experienced by raising my kids with their mom against whatever could have been experienced or gained by leaving them behind for whatever seemed better for me in a moment. When I do, I am left with no explanation of why any dad would cheat themselves of the wonder.

My first best friend, Jim Crew, had the same family situation I did in 1978. His dad left their family years before mine, and we were both being raised by moms facing the world crashing down on them.

Through the years, Jim insisted he would never have kids for fear, he said, they would turn out like him. In spite of his adolescent determinations, my friend turned out pretty average, settling down with a wife followed by the four kids he swore he'd never have.

He wore his adoration for them on his sleeve. And everywhere else.

One night when I was back in my hometown, we met for coffee. Speaking as veterans of dadhood, we exchanged stories and frustrations and surprises discovered along the way. At some point, we also drew inevitable comparisons to the love we had for being dads to the evident distaste our own had for the same calling.

One of the surprises we both shared, he expressed best. My old friend looked at me and said, *"After having kids, I have absolutely no idea how my dad could have left us."*

My arms flopped to my side, my eyes widened, and I blurted out, *"I know!"* For some reason, I was relieved I hadn't been the only one to stumble over the conundrum.

I'm more or less a grown-up now, and, as a pastor, have had far too many close encounters with other people's life and marriage disasters. Consequently, I'm no longer so naive as to think being a dad will always be reason enough for someone to endure abject torment from life's other fronts. I know that there is personal misery I have not experienced that people say trump the reward of being a parent.

I've heard it; I've been told. And yet, I wonder ...

Like all kids, mine usually forget Fathers' Day until the very last moment; I'm pretty sure my son will never remember it on his own.

However, whether the gifts were thoughtful or hasty, I received one of the best last year from my oldest daughter, Madison. It only reinforces my uncertainty about the wisdom of abandoning the joy of parenthood for the sparkle of anything else.

She gave me something usually not associated with Father's Day. Most gifts for dad are manly, something we can play, build, or burp; occasionally we'll get something to spiff up our wardrobe and make us less embarrassing in public.

Madison gave me a flattened flower.

And then, she explained it to me.

Mad got her first phone call from a boy when she was around 13. After it came, I asked her to go with me on a drive to look for pheasants. As I drove slowly over gravel roads, we talked about dating and boys and most details thereof in between spotting roosters.

I made clear that no boy on the planet wanted to have a Bible study with her and that boys were deviant enough to use the very promise of a Bible study—or prayer—or studying—or going to church—or serving in a homeless shelter—or eating potato chips—or anything at all—to get what they were really after. I told her, like all of you have told your appropriately aged daughters, that I know this from personal experience, being such a recovering deviant myself.

At this point in her life, I continued, there was no boy who loved her more than I and no one on earth who more earnestly desired her lifelong happiness. Key to that future happiness, I said, was shelving "romance" for now.

She listened as we lazily made our way across the serpentine road infested with pheasants. To this day when I want to talk to her about serious stuff, I say, *"Let's go look for pheasants."* She knows what that means.

Back to the flower.

After our pheasant talk, the boy caller bought Madison a rose for Christmas. To help drive home the point that my love for her excelled all other earthbound males, I bought her a dozen and had them delivered to her school. Of course, I bought them because I loved her, but having her wannabe boyfriend see them and know the gauntlet for my daughter's heart had been picked up was a nice side benefit.

That was over 6 years ago, and I had forgotten all about it.

Last night before I went to bed, she gave me a card and this pressed rose. I had no idea what it was; she told me she kept those roses I gave her in 2007, put them in a book, and took them to college with her.

She put them on her dorm room wall this last year to remind her of how much I loved her, knowing it was the first and most constant love in her life. This, she said, helped her through the tough stuff of her first year in college.

I didn't know what to say. Who knew looking for pheasants and a few roses could do so much?

I think the most significant things we do in others' lives happen in the very moments we forget the quickest. Because of this, redemption lies hidden all around us in the lives of people we stayed for or encouraged once or prayed over or simply noticed.

Quite honestly, Fathers's Day still feels a little bittersweet. I suppose that's because I've never found an answer for how any dad could excuse himself from the joy of his own kids. There is also a twelve-year-old boy who has been with me since 1978 who insists I never find the answer.

But in a simple card and two-dimensional flower that was pressed in a book for six years my own daughter made all the lost Father's Days of my youth melt away. Her gift reminded me how the Lord is able to exchange beauty for ashes when I least expect it.

And I think the twelve-year-old inside, chained to a moment of sadness for thirty-five years, smiled freely for a brief moment.

My Son Loves Me

"Yes! You? Great!"

I live with the kid and hadn't told him I was subbing for his 8th grade Bible teacher.

In addition to the church I've pastored for twenty years, I started a new job this September teaching 12th grade Bible at our kids' Christian school as a way to afford the tuition that had been raised over the summer. The second day of classes, the eighth-grade teacher asked me to fill in for her while she took another group on a field trip to the Little Big Horn Battlefield where, as Chevy Chase would say, *"Generalissimo George Custer is still dead."*

I hesitated at first. I don't have to teach on Fridays, and she wanted me to come in on my day off when I would normally be fishing, but being the new guy, I thought better of my reflexive refusal.

"Hey guys, my dad's our sub ... yeah, it's my dad."

I looked up from the notes I made for the day to see Hayden in the hall with his friends nodding at me. He was wearing his apparently shrinking, definitely threadbare Nebraska hoodie and his trademark untied shoe.

That's my son.

I introduced myself to the class as Mr. Van Winkle—Pastor of Fellowship Baptist Church. Or, I said, they could call me what Hayden does at home: "Most High Reverend." They laughed; that's good.

Ten boys and two very lonely looking girls stared back at me. I knew a few from sports and a couple from their families who were former church attenders. Eighth graders, every one of them; does anyone remember eighth grade?

I remember flannel shirts, acne, and the first time I ever felt a need to shower every day. Mostly, I remember eighth grade as the adolescent waiting room between the first and the last year of junior high where nothing of significance ever happened. (When I was a kid, jr. high was grades 7–9 and there was no such thing as middle school).

I administered the weekly Bible memory quiz as required and then led a discussion about some verses the teacher left for me to cover. Her goal was to get these fading 13-year-olds to be more open and demonstrative in their public worship. She wanted these grizzled veterans of pubescent awkwardness to cast off adolescent timidity to boldly praise and thank the Lord in the midst of the brethren and among the congregation of the redeemed.

In other words, she wanted a miracle.

It was a good class; I enjoyed myself. When it was over, I asked them to name three things—*not* sports related—for which they were thankful. I got: church, blueberry muffins, and something sports-related (from one of the girls, which made me like her instantly).

Dismissing everyone, I stopped to gather my things and head for the creek where the trout were probably wondering where I was. As the lumbering cluster of boys shuffled past me, I heard a familiar call.

"Love you ..."

Hayden's voice raised in the crowd of his friends and then faded into the busy hallway, swept away by the current of students going to their next class in the undersized corridor. We say it all the time to each other, but this made me pause.

I stopped and sat down. I thought for a second. I leaned back in the chair at the desk; the trout were forgotten.

I've had some family gack on my plate recently.

It's the kind that reaches into me and makes an eternity in the abyss seem like a tropical getaway. Everyone in my vocation, I suppose, has had these types of disasters flopped onto their lap and tangled with righteous impulses to address the situation in unholy ways.

But who hasn't had days where reports of what has happened or what has been revealed caused us to drop and wonder how such things can be, how any person can mangle the lives of those they love and hide it so masterfully?

The fruit of a poisoned family tree does not often reveal itself until it is beyond repair and has burned through a promising life like a virulent plague through a Third World village. Sometimes, when I have seen such evil mutilate hope and love in a life that tried so hard, I tremble.

Sometimes, I just go ahead and cry.

Trafficking in such things recently, I battled being crushed, knowing how my life—a life that is imperfect on its best day— forms and forges the lives-in-progress under my roof. Times had come when I was tormented by the mistakes I know I've made as a dad and paralyzed by the ones I haven't recognized that haunt generations: the kind that are only revealed decades later in ugly letters and behaviors noticed first as annoyances and then as patterns and then as pathologies.

After decades in a career that often calls me to wade through the unrelenting regret people lug around, I know lives of such sadness and dysfunction are never planned; they are the bill come due of days and decisions now lost to time.

Knowing this makes me look back with anxiousness at the me who no longer exists and my kids who are now vanishing into adulthood. Doing so, I offer up a silent, desperate prayer that they will turn around one day and bless their parents, not blame them—love their dad, not hate him.

I've heard a lot of that kind of vitriol lately—a lot. I've listened to stories untold and memories exhumed and watched as these events, now unchained, remake the emotional and religious DNA of people before my eyes. Wails of anger over wrongs long ago and shameful episodes buried like toxic waste so deep in the past people hoped they could no longer do harm have been screamed at me over my phone. I've relived abuses dismissed for years, regrets inexpressible by words, and watched the puzzlement of people who begin remembering traumas like they were a horror movie they had wiped from memory.

I've found the Lord encourages me most in the simplest words and surprising phrases casually dropped; they're like notes of comfort from a watchful dad discovered in your mailbox or sack lunch. His notes are usually delivered just as fear begins to choke me with despair, and they give me hope that my mistakes can always be redeemed by His grace and care.

The voice of my own son delivered the Father's note on this day. Here, unexpectedly, was hope that the honest missteps I've made won't condemn my kids to a lifetime of seething bitterness bubbling just beneath the surface of their crippled emotions. Two words gave me hope that my love for my kids has been well expressed, that my wonder at their brilliance has been evident, that my joy over them has been constant, and my discipline has been received as just and fair.

I have hope my kids love me.

"Yes! You? Great!"

"Hey guys! My dad's our sub ... yeah, it's my dad."

"Love you..."

Pretty insignificant words; they have been lost to the echoes of words spoken in that building today. No one will remember a single syllable of them, except me.

With those words, after this week, I sat and relished how my son was excited and maybe even a little proud that I was the sub—how many eighth graders brag to their friends that dad is the new guy? I thought about how, even with the throng of friends surrounding him, he didn't hesitate to give me our usual *"Love you"* without compulsion or embarrassment.

Peach-fuzz, pimples, and peeps be hanged: my son loves me. I know too many dads who can't say that with confidence; too many kids would rather die than say it at all.

"Love you ..."

It's the Lord's timely grace given to parents, and I soaked it in like cleansing, cascading showers of sunlight after a nuclear winter; no balm in Gilead could have made me feel any better.

My son loves me.

The Ghosts of 68th Street

It was an amazing moment. Not so much in that it was planned or that it was a destination, it was amazing in how unexpected the wave was that swept over me. I had been here before; I had lived here before. But sitting in my late-model Suburban parked along the curb, I realized how long it had been since I had stopped here.

It was 68th Street in Lincoln, Nebraska—710 North 68th Street, to be precise. I spent a chunk of my childhood there. The chunk was big enough and long enough ago that the more monumental moments which shaped me occurred in this neighborhood.

Along with the moments, some of the fondest memories of innocence that continue to play in my mind happened here. My mom, sister, and I moved away twenty-five years ago, but the street was largely the same, the houses unchanged, the washed-out gray asphalt still carpeted the street. Even some of the same people were living in the same houses; the trees seemed not to have grown since we left.

68th Street was and is awash in boxy, brick houses that resemble the company home of the industrial Northeast in terms of uniformity, as if the lower middle-class tide had dumped them on the shore of the avenue. They are square with spartan concrete stoops ascending to a door carved into the brick that opens into the living room; there are no porches or entry areas in these plain-label houses.

The same upstairs floor plan marks each one, and they all have cinderblock basements. This is where the upstairs uniformity ended. Some were overlaid in shag; some had sterile, cold-war bomb shelters; some resembled cellars; some were completely finished; some were partitioned off into hasty bedrooms for teenagers or accidents.

How many stories these brick boxes warehouse is a closely guarded secret. In the time I lived there, Vietnam raged, Nixon resigned, America turned 200, and my dad left us.

But the memories came so easily on this warm summer day. This was the place where I had won dozens of National Championships for the Nebraska Cornhuskers. My stadium was the street, and my friend Jerry Myers and I would put together schedules on notebook paper and play them out on the pavement in front of our houses. We were the only players in our games, throwing passes and tossing option pitches to ourselves against unseen defenses.

We spent the currency of our youth winning the game and hauling home glory.

I can see boys wearing towels around their necks, running through the neighborhood fighting crime with their "capes" flapping behind them. It was here that I saved the universe on galactic missions that made me not only the hero of the entire state of Nebraska but of the galaxy as well.

Forts were hidden in skinny rows of droopy pine trees along wilting metal fences, and secret paths laced throughout backyards and bushes connected the neighborhood like the Ho Chi Minh Trail. Kids traveled these lanes in preference to the sidewalk along the street.

I could probably still make it from one end of the block to the other and never see pavement. It all seemed so big back then.

It was around noon when I relived these memories, but my eyes saw the deepening azure sky between the telephone poles at dusk as another summer's day lilted toward the sunset in the late seventies. If I listened close enough, I could still hear my mom calling me home for dinner; afterward, the locusts begin their serenade, and we walk down to Dairy Queen.

In the midst of this summer afternoon, I could feel the icy tingle of snowflakes hitting my cheeks as I shoveled the driveway clear of drifts beneath the warm, festive glow of Christmas lights around our roof and windows. It was all so real; it was all so haunting; it was all so strangely appealing, comforting.

It was me remembering me.

I saw the people now living in the house I knew as home. I felt as though I was *letting* them live there, as though that house should be mine. Because the events that occurred while we lived there are so personal, because so much of what happened within those walls shaped me and constructed my perspective and grew my dreams, it seemed wrong that anyone else should violate that hallowed ground.

But there they were.

It was like anyone's childhood home, I suppose. It's littered with memories of different days, different people, and different fears. Childhood homes—for the children—are like vessels carrying them on a journey. Kids are unable to secure their own transportation into life, so they're stuck with the vessel they're assigned.

They can't steer it; they can't order it; they can't fix it. What they do is ride it and, sometimes, simply survive it. If they do, one day, all their experiences there will guide them in plotting their own redemption.

Like I plotted mine.

Redemption in that, as a child in that house, I could look around and sense the chaos and see the tears and feel the hurt, and I determined I wouldn't let it happen to me. I would redeem the experiences for wisdom while architecting my tomorrows. I didn't think in those terms as a twelve-year-old, but it would end up being my overriding goal for life.

That is the nature of redemption. It's taking every sorry experience of life and not allowing them to define you; rather, it's letting the sadness and hurt guide you. Redemption is what makes the mistakes valuable; it's what makes the pain bearable; it's what makes faith in a personal God practical.

Redemption is the only hope of turning pain into the raw material of joy. It's the quiet confidence in devastations, knowing there is a Master plan to your life and that the experiences you face can be harnessed for better things. Those moments, I've found, become either what cripples you with built-in excuses to underachieve and revel in bitterness, or they are what fuels you and drives you to exchange them for wisdom and dreams and love.

The difference is redemption.

I would change many things about my life if given the chance; frustration and regret have been occasional companions over time. But visiting these ghosts of 68th street, I can't help but feel that the frantic pursuit of redemption I began watching my dad drive away on this street decades ago can finally end.

Redemption is mine and redemption has given me all that was lost here when I was a boy.

The kid I see scoring another pretend touchdown on the street of my memory will find himself this evening in a home I recognize. He'll walk through the door and be greeted by either uncertainty or insecurity, haunted by the sound of anger or silence.

I'm going home to the place I always dreamed of and will be greeted by love. My wife loves me, my kids love me, our church loves us, and I love them all.

I take in all the ghosts of 68th Street and feel bad for this young echo of me, knowing what awaits him up those concrete steps. However, as my Suburban pulls away from the curb, I'm so happy for the life he has yet to live and I want to tell him that the joy he hopes is out there is real and better than his wildest dreams I know so well.

But he wouldn't understand now; his comfort foods are holidays, imagination, friends, and hope.

Like my dad before me, I leave this kid behind. I'm able to leave him there, not because of a lie but because of the truth. Truth is, I know that kid's redemption is just around that bend.

Driving away on 68th Street, I take a left at Vine Street and head for the Rocky Mountains. I glance in the rearview mirror a last time with the satisfied smile of someone who just skipped ahead and read the happy ending and knows that kid will be alright.

I can't wait for him to find me.

BIO

....

Steve Van Winkle has served as pastor of Fellowship
Baptist Church in Bozeman, Montana, since 1994. He and his
wife, Cheryl, have been married over twenty-five years and have
three children. Steve has published numerous articles, is an
adjunct faculty member of <u>Boston</u>
<u>Baptist College</u>, and holds an MA from Grace Theological
Seminary.